THE SCRUB JAY
MURDERS

THE SCRUB JAY MURDERS

DANIEL C. ERDELY

ARPress
45 Dan Road Suite 5
Canton, MA 02021

Hotline: 1 (877) 389-2759
Fax: 1 (505) 930-7244

Ordering Information:

Quantity sales. Special discounts are available on quantity purchases by corporations,associations, and others. For details, contact the publisher at the address above.

Printed in the United States of America.

ISBN-13:   Softcover   979-8-89330-216-5
               eBook   979-8-89330-215-8

Library of Congress Control Number: 2024900817

Contents

CHAPTER ONE

This was the morning I realized I was getting old. Yesterday, Diane, my wife and I had our usual workout session with Nikki, our trainer. Ordinarily the next day I might feel a little stiff, but today I feel more like I'd been hit by a speeding semi. Despite the fact, with every part of my body in agony, I remembered that I had promised to meet my next-door neighbor, Jerry, who was interested in going for a "bird" walk with me.

My name is Dan and for most of my seventy years I have had this fascination with and love of birds. We had become very involved with birding organizations when we lived in New Jersey and had the opportunity to bird with and learn from the masters of the craft. As a result, in our new Florida home Diane and I have become the "bird" people of our community. Whenever a strange bird was encountered, neighbors would call either Diane or myself for an identification of the stranger.

Today I had promised to introduce Jerry to the wonders of nature that surrounded us in our community. I hoped my body was able to keep up with Jerry, who was an enthusiastic youngster of barely sixty years old. Jeremy and his wife, Melanie, had moved next door to us about two years ago from Wisconsin. Unfortunately, Melanie had a heart attack while on the golf course and had died about a year ago.

Jerry took it very hard and only recently had he started to rejoin the world.

I climbed out of bed slowly hoping my limbs were still able to function. After washing up and with two cups of extra strong coffee, I felt revived enough to give Jerry a call. I asked him to meet me out front. Diane was still in bed and only managed a feeble goodbye and good luck. After teaching for thirty years, she deserved to stay in bed for as long as she wished.

Jerry was excited and anxious to get going on our little adventure. He had recently purchased new high- powered binoculars as well as a huge telephoto lens for his camera. I could tell he had convinced himself that he was going to take the most magnificent bird pictures ever seen by humanity. I had tried to get Jerry interested in bird watching as a way of overcoming his depression. I finally succeeded and admit that I was pleased and surprised by his newly aroused enthusiasm.

We boarded the car and drove to a nearby wooded area that was a state game preserve. Since it wasn't deer hunting season, I was fairly certain we wouldn't end up as target practice for some would be hunter, or so I hoped. Jerry told me that he appreciated my support during the days following his wife's passing.

I'd been here many times before and felt comfortable that we would be able to come up with a decent number of interesting birds. I always found it exciting to introduce a novice to a pastime I truly love. Jerry's enthusiasm was working to reinvigorate my sore limbs. I was confident I could get him hooked on "birding." It was good to see him embrace life once more.

The area was huge, covering a couple thousand acres of lush oak, scrub oak, cypress domes and pine woods. There were trails throughout and it could be very easy to get lost. I always stuck to the main trail and would only venture a little way down a side trail being careful to stay close to my original route. My wife often joked that I totally lacked any sense of direction. I could (and did) get lost in a supermarket. She usually took on the role of navigator on our birding adventures. Today without her presence, I admit to feeling a touch apprehensive. I was hoping that Jerry's navigational skills would be better than mine.

We parked the car under the shade of tall shrubs surrounding the small parking area. The Florida sun could and probably would, be brutal by lunchtime. We planned on spending a couple of hours in the morning. Long before the heat would become unbearable. Even though the calendar said the middle of September, in Florida, it was still summer. I always try to get all my outside activities done before noon. The afternoons were for inside activities.

Jerry was loaded down with all his gear. He had his binoculars hanging around his neck and the camera with the new huge lens dangling from his left hand. His cargo pants were stuffed with bird books, notebooks and bug spray. I silently hoped he also had a compass somewhere in that collection. I carried my old reliable binoculars and my notebook to keep track of our observations. Diane was always sure to leave out sunscreen and had conditioned me to put it on every time I ventured outdoors. She would often say that if she had become a dermatologist, she would want to practice in Florida.

We started down the main trail. Immediately, I indicated that Jerry should look up because right above us in a kettle of vultures was a magnificent adult bald eagle. Watching an eagle soar is always a thrilling sight. The eagle and the vultures were soaring on the air thermals and looked as if they are floating in the sky. Jerry was thrilled and using his new binoculars was able to see more detail. I pointed out to him that there were two kinds of vulture present in the group, turkey vultures and the smaller black vulture. He kept saying "Wow, wow" so I knew he would soon get totally engaged with birding.

Birding is the kind of pastime a person can get hooked on very easily after witnessing the majestic beauty of these avian wonders. I could see that Jerry was destined to become a birder for life. It was fun to bird with an enthusiastic novice.

He fussed with his camera and attempted to take pictures of the eagle in flight. Every time he got the bird in clear focus, it drifted away. I let him try, knowing how challenging it would be to get a clear picture with the bird so high up and drifting aimlessly with the air currents. I suggested we move on down the trail to see what else we could find.

We made our way down the trail into an area of thick vegetation. I heard the familiar call, "drink your tea", of the Eastern or Rufous Sided Towhee. I could just glimpse some movement on the bottom of this thicket. The towhee is a member of the Sparrow family and usually stays low on the ground in thick vegetation. A handsome bird smaller than a robin and with a distinctive and attractive rufous colored side, the Towhee is relatively common in Florida and yet can be elusive to a non-birder.

I called Jerry who had ventured about ten feet ahead of me to come and try to find the bird. We stood squinting alternately with our eyes and binoculars to peer through the thick bushes trying to relocate the bird. I took out my copy of David Sibley's guidebook to show Jerry a picture. I was hoping that the bird would reappear. We searched for about ten minutes without success. Birders learn they often "miss" their target when trying to find birds and unfortunately Jerry's discovery of the Rufous Sided Towhee would have to wait on another day.

We continued our way through the lush thicket. The trail was narrow, and Jerry had again gone ahead on the path. In front of me, I suddenly saw movement in the thicket. It was not a bird. At first, I surmised that we frightened a deer or perhaps a wild boar. I stood very still holding my breath. If it was a boar between us it could mean danger. I realized that I'd had better warn Jerry. I could not see because of the curving of the trail. Boars can be extremely unpredictable and dangerous particularly if there are piglets involved. I was about to call out to him when I heard the shot. Simultaneously, I yelled "Duck" to Jerry who, I feared, might be in range of the gunshot.

My heart was beating fast. I hoped Jerry's inaugural birding experience didn't include getting shot at. Suddenly Jerry reappeared and said, "Where?' I thought he was referring to the gunshot fired near us, but instead he wanted to know the location of the duck. "What duck and where is it?" I was convinced now that even under the threat of gunfire, Jerry, whose concern was in finding the "duck" without any apprehension over the sound of the gunshot, was going to become a great birder. Finally, refocused on the gunshot, we both felt a bit apprehensive. At least I did.

The shot was very near where we were located. Also, there was absolutely no reason someone should be out here hunting. One of the reasons I chose to bring Jerry here was because of its location, very near to our homes, and because this time of year there should be no hunting in the area. I hoped that perhaps it was only someone out hunting boars. There is no season on wild boars so they can be hunted year around. However, it was highly unusual as well as unprofessional for a hunter to be shooting so near a public trail in broad daylight.

Jerry didn't seem the least bit concerned and was ready and eager to proceed along the trail in search of birds.

I thought about it awhile and decided it seemed as if the danger was over and we were not the targets. We may as well bird awhile longer I said to myself. We only had an hour or so left in the morning and the temperature was not yet unbearable. We decided to continue up the trail a while longer.

The foliage on both sides of the narrow trail was thick and impenetrable in this area. We heard birds in the undergrowth that were impossible to flush into visibility. "Let's move on to the clearing up ahead," I suggested.

In the back of my mind though was the thought that something was not quite right. I tried to dispel my discomfort, however, and locate some birds for Jerry.

CHAPTER TWO

We walked forward around the curve in the path and entered an area with a little more openness. On the path in front of us about thirty or forty feet away I saw three birds on the ground picking on seeds from nearby plants. Bobwhites! I quietly got Jerry's attention to these birds, and we stood quite still watching them as they foraged in the weeds.

Bobwhites are chunky, dark ruddy brown birds. They are usually quite shy and often are difficult to locate. They can fly but prefer to amble on the ground looking for tasty plants and seeds. In recent years they have declined immensely in number. In our area, it is now a rare treat to find them. When Diane and I first moved to our nearby home we could still see them running in our yard, but because of habitat loss, they have been mostly driven away. I told Jerry this was really his lucky day! Finding a Bobwhite out in the open is special.

At first the birds seemed oblivious to us but as Jerry clicked away on his camera the birds recognized our presence and moved into the taller nearby vegetation and disappeared.

Jerry was ecstatic! He was confident he had taken the definitive photo of the Eastern Bobwhite!

We cautiously moved forward towards where the bobwhites had been feeding. We looked carefully through the tall foliage around us hoping for another glimpse of the birds. I stopped suddenly. In the area on the right side of the path there was something large lying under some scrub oaks. From where I stood it seemed to be an article of clothing and under another bush, I thought I could make out what looked like a shoe.

My first thought was that these items of clothing were probably discarded and left there by some hunter or perhaps were abandoned after a romantic tryst. I couldn't imagine making love under the scrub oaks with the dirt, bugs, and possibly even a snake around. I guess at seventy my sense of romanticism has mellowed to the point it requires soft pillows and air conditioning. I started going forward on the path, but an inner voice told me to go back and just look at the clothing up close. It was a man's jacket. Under another bush was a shoe. This must have been a doozy romantic tryst, I thought to myself. It was then I saw it. Near the top of a nearby oak tree sat a magnificent Scrub Jay. It was looking down at me probably wondering about this intrusion into their homeland and hoping there might be peanuts! I was excited that on his initial birding experience Jerry was able to enjoy seeing this fabulous bird.

Scrub Jays are a Florida specialty. This sub-species of the Jay family of birds can be found only in the sunshine state. They are unique and specialized. This sub species is a beautiful, almost tame and fearless bird that lives in family colonies only in central Florida. It has a distinctive pale blue and gray plumage that is unmistakable. About the size of a Blue Jay, the bird's precarious survival is entirely dependent on man's intervention. It lives only in scrub oak of a certain size intermingled with saw palmetto, low pines and sandy soil. In the past lightning strikes would ignite the fires necessary to keep the scrub at the required height. Today, managed burns are necessary to provide the correct scrub size. Without man's intervention the bird would not be able to survive. As a result of being classified as an endangered species, the birds are banded with individualized band patterns. Surprisingly, only two of the birds I saw were banded. The two other birds did not have bands. I speculated that they must be last year's young and the naturalist had not yet been here. The habitat management requires that tracts of land must have controlled burns to maintain the necessary height requirements to insure the colonies survival. I had not suspected that there might be a colony of Scrub Jays nearby. Scrub Jay colonies are identified and under the supervision of the Florida Fish and Wildlife Agency. I knew one of the naturalists involved in monitoring the populations of the bird but was not aware that a colony was so near my home.

It was gratifying to find this rare species of bird on Jerry's inaugural birding expedition. Jerry should buy lottery tickets today.

Jerry was ecstatic. Finding the bobwhites and then seeing the Jays was like winning the lottery. Scrub Jays don't mind human company and we were able to observe five birds. They seemed to be posing for Jerry enabling him to take as many photos as he wanted. Unfortunately, their tameness can occasionally be detrimental to the birds. Many well-intentioned people bring peanuts to feed them which can make them very vulnerable to predation from birds of prey. Hawks would have an easy time preying on an exposed Jay.

I had almost forgotten that my original intention was to go and look more closely at what was under the trees there. I carefully and quietly moved forward towards the trees. The birds started to react to my approach with nervous bobs and jerks. Subsequently as I neared them, the birds dropped into the dense undergrowth and disappeared. I heard Jerry whisper, "Oh shit. They're gone." I found a stick nearby that I could use to retrieve the clothing and the shoe.

I was very careful to look for snakes. This area has pygmy rattlesnakes which are small and can be concealed under leaves or grass. There are other snakes as well including coral snakes and timber rattlesnakes. I remember hearing that there were six kinds of poisonous snakes one could encounter in Florida. I was eager to avoid any snake! I reminded Jerry to stay on the path and wait for me. I didn't want him to end up getting bitten by a snake. I moved carefully through the low brush always on the lookout for snakes.

I love being out in nature, but I admit, I hate snakes. It's probably a typical reaction most people share. I realize that snakes make a valuable contribution to the circle of life, but I'm still wary of them and would rather not have an encounter with one. I am as wary of garter snakes as I am of rattlers.

As I got nearer, I realized that there was more to this than just a shirt and a shoe. I poked at it and jumped. It was in fact a body! I stood there completely bewildered. I was so focused on the Jays that I didn't see that there was more there than just a shoe. I also had missed the fact that there were drag marks on the ground and footprints nearby. For fear of tampering with the scene I quickly returned to where Jerry was waiting for me. He was happily looking at all his photos. "I got some really outstanding photos," he boasted.

I nervously told Jerry about finding the body. His glee over seeing the Jays was short lived. Stunned, we both moved quickly back to the car. My cell phone was out of range. We had to inform the sheriff's department. Jerry was confident that his phone would work. We got to the car, and I dialed 911 using his phone. I told them about finding a body and that we would be waiting at the trail entrance.

I was totally confused and upset. Questions kept coming to mind. For example, did I even know for sure if the person was dead? Why didn't I take the time to find out? I was so shaken that I neglected to really look through the dense cover to examine the body. Besides hearing the gunshot, did I see or hear anything else? I had always thought of myself, as a result of my birding skills, extremely alert and attentive to everything around me. Yet now, I was not sure of anything. I'd been out in the woods on frequent birding adventures and never imagined anything like this before.

My mind was racing as I considered what to do next. It bothered me that I wasn't even sure the victim was deceased. My body was shaking as we waited for the sheriff to arrive. I don't believe I ever perspired as much. My shirt was totally soaked. We stood at the head of the path and anxiously waited. There were no other vehicles in the parking area. We were probably the only witnesses, except for the shooter, to what had happened.

Jerry was babbling that perhaps the person had a heart attack and was not the victim of a shooting. He seemed somewhat excited by the day's events. First the birds and now the mystery of the shooting would make this an adventure he would never forget.

CHAPTER THREE

I paced nervously looking in both directions for the sheriff. It seemed like an eternity, but after fifteen minutes the sirens announced their arrival. Two cars pulled into the parking area and were immediately followed by an ambulance. Jerry had suddenly become very pale and quiet and was fidgeting with his binoculars. I was beginning to think it was good the ambulance came so quickly because he might need it.

Two deputies emerged from their cars and were immediately followed by three EMT's from the ambulance. One of the deputies showed me his ID and asked me to lead the way. The EMTs, two young men and a youngish female followed carrying a stretcher.

We wound our way down the trail oblivious to the chatter of the birds around us. It seemed that now the birds were suddenly active and displaying. It was almost as if they were now taunting us that we couldn't take the time to find them.

Soon more sheriff vehicles arrived. It seemed like a small army of law officers descended on the area. We arrived at the sight where the body was located. The EMTs went right to work examining the body. It was officially determined that the individual was deceased. Another man wearing a sport coat and tie stepped forward to examine the corpse. Two other non-uniformed men stepped up and started to assume control. They directed the officers to tape off the area and cordon off access to the park. An officer pointed us out to the men. I assumed after watching innumerable detective shows on TV that the two men were detectives who had begun an investigation. After talking to the man who had examined the body, it was apparent that it was determined this was murder.

Jerry, very quiet and somber looking was at the back of the line. I'm sure he never expected this on his premier birding outing.

All of us were totally silent, focused on the gruesome task in front of us. We strode forward to the patch of scrub oak. I saw the lookout Jay sound off to warn the clan to get down. The Jays curiosity was evident as they occasionally would show themselves intrigued by the crowd of deputies that had invaded their domain.

The deputy bent over and looked at the body. His partner took pictures as they lifted the foliage to get a clearer view. The body was face down. It had a tan blood-soaked short sleeved shirt, tan cargo shorts and on the feet were fancy hiking boots. From where I stood, far behind the deputies and the EMTs, I couldn't tell for certain if the victim was male or female. There was a lot of blood still moist on the ground also.

After finishing the exam of the crime scene, the EMTs folded out the stretcher and pulled the body out from the vegetation. They turned it over and I could see that it was a male about forty or fifty years old with salt and pepper hair, a ruddy complexion and there was a tattoo on the left arm of an eagle. I wondered if this victim could be a fellow bird watcher and was the shooting directed at bird watchers. Was it possible that Jerry and I could have been potential victims? A chilling thought.

After they had finished the preliminary search of the area, we headed back to the parking area behind the ambulance crew carrying the body. The head deputy walked beside me and introduced himself as Deputy Nick Nicotra. He was of medium build with gray hair and a solid looking demeanor. You knew immediately he was experienced and competent. When we reached the parking area while the ambulance crew loaded the body aboard, he gave muted directions to the other deputies. Two of them went back on the trail camera in hand while the third a young female deputy roped the path and parking area off with the yellow, Do Not Enter ribbon.

When he came back to us, he asked for our names and addresses and why we had come to this location. He looked at our equipment and asked if while we were doing our bird watching had we seen or heard anyone else. He asked us to recall in detail the entire unfolding of events. When we had finished, he told us we could leave but that we should expect a visit or call from him later in the day. Jerry and I drove back to our development in silence.

I dropped Jerry off at his home and wondered if he'd ever dare go birding with me again. We said our good-byes and I drove anxiously back to my home. I knew that Diane would be upset. I told her we'd be back by lunchtime. It was now late in the afternoon. As I walked to my front door, I could see the faces of my two corgis pressed against the glass ready to greet me. I was sure Diane would think that we had gotten ourselves lost in the woods knowing my lack of navigation skills, but at least Moto and Sweetie were ready to welcome me without hesitation or judgement.

When I walked in the door and was greeted profusely by the two spoiled canines, I saw the look of relief in Diane's eyes. She told me she had been convinced we were horribly lost and that she was preparing to organize search parties to try and find us. She gave me a kiss and waited for the explanation.

I reviewed the entire sequence of events, and she showed great concern. She also wondered if bird watchers weren't the target. I pointed out that while the victim looked like a bird watcher, he did not have any optical equipment with him. We puzzled over it awhile exchanging different theories before deciding to eat. It's better to think on a full stomach.

Afterwards, we washed up the dishes, fed the two barking hooligans and were about to sit down when the doorbell rang. I looked out and saw Deputy Nicotra standing there with a serious expression. He was accompanied by a younger man with a bushy mustache and a serious demeanor. I invited the two detectives in, introduced him to Diane and the two corgis and we went into the Florida room to sit down.

Deputy Nicotra was about sixty years old and was a retired police detective from New York City. He relocated to Florida a couple of years before and after a few months of idleness decided he needed to get back to work. He thought about working for Disney in security, but by fate he was introduced to Sheriff Grady, the Polk County Sheriff, at an event in our community. The rest is obvious. He was needed and the Sheriff was very pleased to welcome Nicotra's experience to his team.

His partner was Detective John Smiley whose facial expression did not correspond to his name. He was handsome in a strange sort of way with blond hair and an ample blond mustache. His blue eyes were piercing and belied a serious nature.

Deputy Nicotra asked me once more to go over all the details of us finding the body. He told us that they had been able to identify the victim as Robert Hatch of nearby Haines City. He also informed us that Mr. Hatch was indeed a bird watcher and according to his wife, was hardly ever separated from his very expensive binoculars. He inquired if we had seen the binoculars. They had not been able to find them at the scene and speculated that the motive might have been robbery. I thought that Jerry and I with our optical equipment and his fancy camera, could easily have been a target too. He told me to call him immediately if we thought of anything else, however insignificant it might seem. Anything that could help in the investigation would be appreciated.

After he left, Diane and I sat there quietly taking in all we had learned. Our seriousness was interrupted by Moto and Sweetie reminding us it was time for their nightly walk before bedtime. Dogs have a way of comforting and reminding us that we are loved. We leashed the dogs and went on a long walk, listening on the way with birds singing their night songs. We were hoping to hear the barred owl call out to announce his presence.

CHAPTER FOUR

I woke up the next morning after having a restless night contemplating all that had happened the last twenty- four hours. It was seven fifteen. I was surprised to find that Diane, who usually sleeps until at least eight, was not in bed. The corgis were also not in the room. Still in my sleep boxers, I crept out into the hall and saw the two dogs wolfing down their breakfasts and I heard clicking from the office which meant that Diane was busy at the computer. I went back into the bedroom to do my morning activities and emerged a few minutes later to find Moto and Sweetie looking at me and wanting me to fix their breakfasts. Corgis can be real con artists!

I went into the office, Diane looked up and told me she had found out that the colony of Scrub Jays Jerry and I had found was an "undiscovered" one. Scrub Jays are protected by law and each year after breeding season an inventory is taken of all the birds. Each bird is marked by a series of color-coded bands on their legs and can be readily identified by the naturalists working for their protection. The young birds are counted prior to a bird bander who will individually band them in a way that will identify each one as unique. Diane has often volunteered as a counter. She is aware of all the local colony locations.

The fact that this colony was not listed as a known sight was significant. She asked if we were able to see any bands on the birds we had seen. I told her I didn't recall any, but maybe Jerry's pictures might show if any of the birds were banded. I suddenly recalled that Two of the birds were banded. This probably meant that this was a new colony just recently established.

I knew what was coming. After breakfast Diane suggested we drive out to the site to see the birds. I told her I didn't think that was such a good idea as there was a murderer somewhere nearby. Maybe we should just report to the Fish and Wildlife authorities. Diane, needless to say, didn't like my suggestion. Besides I interjected, the area is still probably closed off and the Sheriff's department is undoubtedly still present there. "I'll get my Fish and Wildlife ID so that I can show them that I need to count the Scrub Jays," she said. After forty-eight years of marriage, I still haven't learned when to give up and just go along with Diane's ideas.

When we got to the site, I was surprised to see that there was no police presence. The only reminder was a bit of the Do Not Enter tape still hanging from a nearby tree. We parked the car and I once again suggested that maybe the murderer was still around and waiting for the next victim. Her reply was that the perpetrator now had a good pair of binoculars and was probably far away. He would never come back here. I hoped she was right.

We went up the path and I could hear a Pileated Woodpecker in the distance with his raucous keekeekeekeekuk call reverberating through the woods. We soon made the turn onto the scrubby more open area where the jays lived. Cautiously we looked around and then they appeared. Three jays appeared sitting on the tallest scrub oak, waiting to see what happened next. While Diane tried to identify the birds from their bands, I looked around at the site where the body was found. All that remained was the drag marks through the leaves and dirt. I kept an eye out for any suspicious movement or for any strange sounds.

After Diane had finished her observations, we started our way back to the parking area. That's when I saw it. Amid some tall trees and thick vegetation near the top of the tallest tree and hidden from sight was a deer stand. It had a direct view of the area where the murder had occurred. Could the murderer have been there waiting for his victim or victims? Maybe Jerry and I had been extremely lucky. Mr. Hatch, the shooting victim, had been there before us.

When we got back home, Diane went to the office to E Mail her findings to the head of the Scrub Jay project while I called Deputy Nicotra. He answered immediately. When I told him about the deer stand, he said he'd be right over. There was nothing in yesterday's report that mentioned a deer stand. Less than fifteen minutes later, the Corgis announced his arrival.

He first commented that he was surprised we had returned to the crime scene. He always suspected that birders could sometimes do strange things in pursuit of their avian activities. Going back to the scene of the murder the day after a shooting had taken place there, proved it he thought. He then asked us to get in the car with him to show him exactly where the deer stand was located. After we had done this, he indicated surprise that his investigators had overlooked this. He thanked us and drove us home. Diane was convinced that neighbors, who may have seen us get in and out of a Sheriffs vehicle, were now completely sure there was something criminal about us. A few of our neighbors regarded bird watching as a strange hobby pursued by strange people. This was like my view that golf was a strange sport. It was pursued by some strange people who thought hitting a little ball with a club was a fun exercise. At least bird watchers walked and did not rely on little carts to get around.

We spent the rest of the day and evening playing a game of speculation. Why would someone want to murder a bird watcher? Was it to steal the optics or was it more sinister?

CHAPTER FIVE

The next day, Diane and I decided to try to put the whole thing behind us. As best we could, we would spend the day enjoying our dogs by taking them for an outing to the dog park. Moto, our male corgi, especially loved running and playing fetch. He relished running like the wind to catch the tennis ball. Sweetie, the female, was an explorer. She would cover every inch of the dog park reading every communication that other dogs left behind. She also loved socializing with any other dog in the park. We spent over an hour with the dogs before heading for home.

Driving past the nature preserve that was the sight of the murder, Diane noticed a young man dressed all in camouflage with a pair of binoculars around his neck entering the trail. "Stop," she yelled, "I think you'd better call that detective right away."

"He's probably just there to bird. These young guys are very often passionate bird watchers," I replied.

"Yea, but they usually aren't carrying guns."

"Are you sure you saw a gun. It probably was something else. There's no car in the parking area. It's just some kid."

She was adamant that it was a gun. She admitted that she wasn't quite sure, but it looked like a gun. We called Detective Nicotra and

Diane told him what she observed. He said he would dispatch patrol cards there immediately he would be there in a few minutes.

I hoped that these daily calls to him were useful and not just a wild goose chase. I didn't want our amateur sleuthing to interfere with real police work.

Detective Nicotra seemed genuinely interested even though I indicated that we weren't positive about the weapon. "Thanks," he said. "We take all calls seriously."

"I'm hungry," I said to Diane. "Let's go to that bakery in Haines City. I heard they have great sandwiches at lunch."

We ate silently. Both of us were unable to stop thinking about all these recent events. We ate quickly and decided to go home immediately. As we drove by the preserve, we saw two patrol cars in the lot with a third car pulling into the parking area.

"Nicotra took our call seriously," Diane said. "See, at least somebody does," she whispered looking at me. Diane turned on the TV as soon as we entered the house to the all-news channel. We were both shocked by what we heard. There was another shooting at a nearby nature preserve that involved one fatality with another victim seriously wounded. Both victims appeared to be bird watchers. More details were promised as the story developed. This incident occurred close by, but in a neighboring county. As a result, our Polk County detectives were not directly participating in the investigation there.

I was convinced these shootings were connected. This could not be just a coincidence. Could it be that someone disliked bird watchers so much? Another more reasonable thought was that these shootings were to steal the expensive binoculars and camera equipment that the victims had on them. In either case, it seemed that bird watching had now become a dangerous pastime.

Still, the distance between locations was not that great, only three miles or so. Coincidence or was there a connection between the shootings?

Could it really be that someone disliked bird watchers so much they would shoot them? Another more reasonable theory was that the theft of expensive camera equipment and optics was the motivation. In either case, it seemed that birding was now dangerous.

I was tense all day. The local all- news station kept repeating the same story without any new information. Diane was curious and told me that this preserve had a wonderful, very successful Scrub Jay population and she had been there several times for the bird count. Did these murders have anything to do with Scrub Jays? Not likely, we agreed. It was probably an attempt to steal expensive optics.

About four in the afternoon the phone rang. It was Nick. He told me that his deputies had not found anyone there. They had been near the deer stand, had searched through all the undergrowth and had not found any sign of the person. He also indicated that he had been in touch with the Sheriff of Osceola County. They had discussed the striking similarities in the shootings and believed that they were related. They both believed, as we did, that robbery was the motive. He told us to be careful when we go out birding.

Corgis have a way of changing a person's focus. Moto and Sweetie weren't interested in the news. They just wanted to play. Sweetie, the older of the two dogs still gets what we like to call the"zoomies", where she races at top speed through the whole house. The dog's antics diffused our anxiety and we were grateful for the new perspective of life you get from having dogs.

We watched the news before turning in and did not learn anything we hadn't heard before except that the victims were from Orlando and were in love with Scrub Jays. Neighbors said they often took peanuts out to the Jay colonies to feed them. They showed a picture of one of them with a Jay sitting on his head.

As I lay in bed, I wondered what the world was coming to now that it seemed as if bird watching was a dangerous activity.

CHAPTER SIX

We woke up early and decided to show our defiance of the threat. We would go bird watching. We were planning to drive to Titusville and bird at Merritt Island and at nearby Canaveral National Seashore. We packed our gear and took off. This is one of our favorite birding spots and almost always has a surprise bird or two. There also are a couple of popular Scrub Jay colonies where many visitors are introduced to the rare and threatened species. Another thing we love about this area is that it has one of our favorite restaurants, The Crossroads, and their delicious rock shrimp.

We drove around the nature trail enjoying views of all the regular egrets herons and ibis and aweing at the beautiful Roseate Spoonbills. We found Avocets, Black Necked Stilts, Common Moorhen, Coots and more. The Bald Eagle was the topper. Majestically perched on the top of a dead tree holding a fish it probably stole from an Osprey. It was a beautiful sight.

After going around the trail we drove to the area where the Scrub Jays were located. We weren't fearful because there almost always are plenty of other birders there enjoying the birds. Feeding the birds is prohibited but there usually is someone there surreptitiously feeding peanuts to the birds. As a result the birds here are very tame and will often land on someone's head. Being so outgoing can be dangerous for the birds as it makes them more vulnerable to predation from hawks.

While observing the birds we met an elderly gentleman, Joe Gruber, who came to see the birds almost every day. He lived in nearby Titusville and while not a professed birder spent a lot of time walking the area and getting to know all about the flora and fauna surrounding it. He was very friendly and talkative. He told us he was originally from South Jersey near Cherry Hill and had moved to Florida about ten years ago. To keep in shape, he walks usually about five to ten miles a day.

Joe told us he learned about the Scrub Jays because on one walk several years ago a bird landed on his head. Ever since he was fascinated with them. He used to bring peanuts to feed them. However, one time was told by a park ranger that it is illegal to do so because of the potential harm it could do to the Jays. He said he often reminds visitors of the no feeding rule.

He told us that there was one guy a few months ago that he described as totally obnoxious. He said this guy seemed to resent the fact that there were other people here. The birds need to be left alone. He often got into verbal spats with visitors over the slightest thing. If you talked too loudly or tried to get too close for photos or God Forbid, you dropped anything on the ground, his wrath was upon you. He didn't know the gentleman's name and was glad he hadn't been around here for a while. I wondered if this guy might have resorted to violence instead of verbal spats. "This guy acted like he would kill you for feeding the Jays, "he commented. "There are, you realize, crazy bird watchers too!"

We chatted for another few minutes, said our goodbyes and looked forward to a late lunch of rock shrimp. A good lunch and a cold beer can do a lot to relax a person.

It was a wonderful day that happily reaffirmed our enjoyment of bird watching and living in Florida.

It's about an hour and a half ride back to our home. It started to rain as we drove. Late afternoon, early evenings Floridians know are prime time for thunderstorms. Florida is known as the lightning capital of the

USA and the storms can be ferocious. This one was very strong with torrential downpours, loud booming thunder and vivid lightning.

Both of us thought about our dogs at home who hated these storms. Sweetie, our female would pace around the house panting trying to find a safe place from the storm. She would often try to squeeze in the smallest, darkest place she could find. Moto wasn't quite as disturbed by the storm but would spend his time alertly looking out the front door window for any sign of our arrival.

It took us longer to get home than we expected because of the ferocity of the storm. I was extremely relieved to turn into our community's gate and off the main highway. We pulled into our driveway and had to wait about ten minutes before the rain subsided enough for us to make a run for the front door. As we approached the door, we could see two noses pressed against the glass eagerly awaiting our arrival and their dinner.

We changed into dry clothes, fed the dogs and noticed that the light on the phone was blinking indicating a message. I listened to the messages and the first was from someone telling me we were in imminent danger of arrest from the IRS and that we should immediately call this number to satisfy this lien. After laughing about it, I listened to the second message. It was from Deputy Nicotra who in a grave voice asked us to call him as soon as possible.

I dialed the number and Diane picked up the extension. When he answered he almost sounded relieved to hear from us. He told us that there had been another murder. This time it was at the Disney Wilderness Preserve in nearby Kissimmee. He was worried that perhaps we had ignored his advice and were birding locally. He didn't give us many details except that the surviving victim of the shooting in Osceola was not able to give any worthwhile information and didn't recall seeing or hearing anything prior to the shooting. He again reminded us to be very alert and careful when we were out looking for birds.

CHAPTER SEVEN

I got up earlier than usual, walked and fed the dogs before scanning the newspaper for any news on the shooting at the Wilderness Preserve. Unfortunately, the article gave no new details. They hadn't even had an identification of the victim and the article gave no indication as to whether the victim was a birder.

I was feeling uneasy and not satisfied with the idea of robbery as a motive. In the last murders there seemed to be no attempt to steal the optics from the victims. If robbery was not the motive, what could it be? Were they just random shootings by some deranged individual? I thought about going back to the sight of the first shooting just to look around once more. I thought if I waited in the parking area until more hikers showed up, I would be safe. Just in case I wouldn't take my binoculars.

When Diane came out of the bedroom, we discussed the latest news. We had breakfast. Diane was going to fool around on her computer looking for any more news or gossip about the shootings. I told her I was going out for a while and immediately she jumped up and confronted me. "Where are you going?" she inquired suspiciously. I don't know how she does it, but she can read my mind. I finally confessed to my plan. She pointedly said she was coming no matter what.

I didn't know exactly what I was looking for, but I knew in my heart that there was something there that everyone had overlooked.

When we got to the parking lot there were two other cars there. I felt more confident that we would be safe with more people in the vicinity. I asked Diane to keep watch near the car. She said no. Diane indicated that she was coming along, adding that she thought I'd get lost without her.

We strode down the path. The birds invariably were everywhere because we were without out binoculars. I heard Brown Headed Nuthatches in the tall pines nearby, a bird I desperately wanted for my year's list. We had no time for birding. When we arrived near the spot where the victim was found, I used a stick to poke around in the tall weeds. Diane was doing the same nearby. Suddenly I heard something behind me. Someone was coming up the trail. I grabbed Diane and we moved behind a tall pine tree and waited.

Deputy Nick appeared. When he saw us we were relieved and he was annoyed. "Yea, I'll bet you're bird- watching ," he bellowed! He said he was driving by and saw our car in the parking area and decided he'd better check on us. I explained my reason for coming and he asked if I had satisfied my inkling. Unfortunately, our search was fruitless.

We started to walk back to the parking area when I saw it. Amidst all the tall grass and almost completely hidden from view a bit of silver flashed. I pointed it out to Nick and all three of us moved the grass and tall underbrush to reveal a bicycle. Had someone hidden a bicycle and gone out on the trail?

Nick said he'd assign a deputy to keep an eye out for the owner of the bike. He warned us again of the danger of being out here. We said goodbye and made our way home.

I wasn't convinced that the bike had anything to do with the murder. It probably was just some young person who was just going for a long walk down the trail and would be surprised when he returned to find a deputy sheriff standing guard over his bike.

Later in the day, we heard that the murder at the Disney Preserve was a domestic incident and not related to the other shootings. At least it was not directed at birders, I thought, feeling some relief.

Part Two: Cal's Story
Chapter Eight

Cal Turner always was a strange kid. His peers in high school tormented him with insults and jabs. Later they ignored him. He had no real friends and found satisfaction by taking long walks often in a nearby nature preserve. His mother was seldom at home preferring the company of men she met at The Green Room, a neighborhood bar. He never knew his father. His only pleasure was in spending time with the birds and animals he found on his walks. He would observe people from a distance and discovered that the woods could be places for sexual rendezvous sometimes better than watching the porn he occasionally saw at the neighborhood adult shop. Cal used a fake ID to get in and even though he looked young the attendant never questioned his age.

Cal had never been a great student. His attendance at school was spotty at best. He only came to school when he felt like it. His mother never paid much attention to the calls from school and never even discussed the situation with Cal.

One time the school social worker made a home visit. Cal's mother who was having a lunch date with Jack Daniels, was incoherent. She was not at all interested in what Mrs. Harvey, the school's child study team head had said about his lack of progress at school.

Mrs. Harvey dutifully had reported the situation to the county child social services bureau, but because Cal was seventeen nothing came of it.

Cal finally decided to quit school altogether after a group of boys decided to use him as a punching bag in the boy's lavatory. They pushed into one of the stalls. One of the boys pulled his pants down and assaulted whatever pride he had left. Wiping away his tears he walked out of the building rubbing his wounds and went into a nearby woods. It was there in the grass he saw a covey of bobwhite. He sat very still and the birds pecked at the ground very near to where he was sitting and totally ignored him. As he watched the birds, he realized that he knew so little about them. He wasn't even sure he knew what kind of bird they were, only that they seemed to be a lot like chickens. The bobwhites had distracted him from his anger enough that even though he wanted revenge, he would wait patiently for a good time and place.

He walked down the main street of town to the library. He'd only been in the library once before when a teacher in elementary school had brought the class here for story time. He walked through the library looking at all the racks of books until he came to a sign that said birds. He browsed through the books on the shelf until he came to one that was titled: A Field Guide to the Birds East of the Rockies. Carefully he paged through the book until he found the picture of the bird he had seen. Bobwhite, he thought, what a strange name for a bird.

He moved behind the shelf with the book in hand. He stuck the book down his pants, pulled his shirt out and walked out the door.

When he got home, he holed himself up in his room and started looking at all the pictures. He remembered seeing the mockingbird in a tree by his house and a cardinal in a bush nearby. He was fascinated by the variety of birds and wanted to go out and find every one of them. His mother never even noticed that he was no longer attending school.

In fact, she rarely acknowledged his presence. If he disappeared one day she would notice when the child support payments stopped.

Day after day he studied from the book. He carried it everywhere he went. Soon he was able to identify by sight and by song all the common birds found in central Florida. He now had a bicycle which he had "found" by a bus stop chained against a light pole. Cutting the chain was easy and he now had a mode of transportation that would expand his horizons.

Cal had found a meaning and a passion to his life that had been missing. He would ride the bike for miles looking for new birding spots. He became a passionate record keeper writing careful notes of when and where he found a particular bird. He learned to identify birds by sound and had become quite skilled in listening skills.

His mother started to take notice especially since there always seemed to be money missing from her pocketbook. She always seemed to have money. He realized she was probably doing business with men during the day while he was at school. He once found a condom in the bathroom but didn't think that much about it. Living here one could expect anything. She thought about confronting him about the missing money, but too much alcohol makes a person forgetful. As a result, Cal was able to pilfer five or ten dollars each day which was enough for him to get a fast-food sandwich for lunch. Cal had become so obsessed with finding and identifying birds that all other reality disappeared. He still harbored a hatred for humanity and found comfort in the birds. He had no qualms about breaking into vehicles stealing valuables. He even managed to pilfer the tip box from the counter of the local pizza shop. Twenty-two dollars would buy him supper for a few days.

The one thing he needed and lacked was a pair of binoculars. He would go in Wal Mart to the sporting goods section and look through the locked glass case at the glasses available. He was thinking about how to get the cashier distracted so he could get a pair, but with store security cameras it seemed too risky.

He came up with another plan. He would go to where a group of birder watchers were gathered and wait for an opportunity for someone to get distracted. He would look through cars in the lot to find an unlocked door. Suddenly, an opportunity presented itself. An elderly women put her glasses in the car and then rushed off to the restroom. He walked nonchalantly to the car, looked all around, saw no one, opened the door and snatched the glasses. He quickly made his way down the trail and out of sight. He now had a pair of binoculars. Top notch Zeiss. The kid had good taste.

Cal got on his bike and rode quickly back to town. He went directly to the lake and took out his stolen binoculars and scanned the lake. He was thrilled that now he was able to see details of the egrets that were not visible with the naked eye. He felt that this justified his stealing the optics. She looked like she could easily afford to replace them and after all he was just a poor deprived kid.

This little heist was easy. Cal wondered why he didn't do this kind of thing before now. He was feeling invincible. I'm too smart to get caught, a little voice whispered in his head. The key was to be patient and not careless.

CHAPTER NINE:

Cal's daily routine was established. Each day he would get on his bike ride to the convenience store nearby and purchase a couple bottles of water, some cookies, maybe an apple, and sometimes pretzels or chips. If possible, he would stuff some of the items into his pockets and only pay for part of the items he picked out. Then fully supplied, he would head to a forested area or a park nearby and hide his bike and bird. He seldom encountered anyone and was perfectly happy avoiding any social contact.

One day he saw a bird he could not identify. His guide book did not seem to have a picture that satisfied his curiosity. He leafed through the entire book and could not find a bird that came close to the one he had seen. He wrote a clear description of the bird he had seen and included noting the location, the type of tree it was on and even a rough description of its call. He knew he needed to go back to the library and look through other books.

The next day, he got on his bike and made his way to the library. He knew exactly where the bird books were kept and started to browse through the books. He knew the bird was of the passerine family. He had learned about the different families of birds and recognized that this bird was somewhat like a blue jay. At first, he thought that this might be just a strange variation of a jay, sort of like a birth defect. However, he soon changed his opinion and decided this must be a special kind of jay.

He picked up a book that was exclusively about the birds of Florida. As he was leafing through the book, he found an exact picture of the bird he was seeking to identify. It was a Florida Scrub Jay. He studied the picture and read the commentary. He was enthralled. Birds had become his escape from reality. Finding a new bird each day became a passion. Finding the Scrub Jay seemed to give him purpose. He would take it upon himself to protect as best he could this endangered species.

Recognizing their vulnerability, he would frequently go to the locations of the birds' colonies and guard them from predation. He came to resent the people who would bring peanuts and try to get the birds to sit on their head or shoulders. Eventually, he even started to yell and curse at those who dared feed his birds. Didn't they understand they were his birds? He spent more and more time consumed with his self-appointed responsibility.

His passion led him back to the library for more bird books. His reading level was limited but his desire to learn more about birds was extraordinary. What he couldn't read could be overcome by the pictures and combined with his outdoor observations made him a very successful birder.

He looked all around where he was standing. The library was crowded today. He wanted to make sure no one would see him putting the book down his pants. When he felt safe, he put the book down in the front of his pants and secured it by sticking it into the elastic of his briefs. He wore an especially long tee shirt that covered the front of his pants down to his hips. No one would notice the book stuffed there.

Someone did notice. A man had come into the book aisle from behind where Cal was standing. He saw the whole thing and being a sheriff's deputy and a detective, he couldn't ignore it. He quickly went over to Cal and stood facing him. He pulled out his ID and told Cal what he had seen and to turn over the book. Cal was confused and distraught. He had never been caught before and was assessing the situation. Detective Smiley was no stranger to dealing with situations like this and was considering letting the young man off the hook with a stern lecture after he had retrieved the book.

Smiley judged that the kid was not being malicious. He needed a fatherly lecture about honesty and responsibility.

Cal suddenly pushed the deputy, and charged down the aisle and ran out the front door. Smiley ran after him briefly before losing sight of the kid as he ran down a side street and disappeared. The detective thought about filing a report, but after speaking to the librarian, decided not to pursue it. He would, however, remember to keep his eyes out for the kid in case he ever saw him again. The young man needed a good talking to, Smiley felt he was the one who could do it.

Cal ran as fast as possible down a side street. When he realized he wasn't being pursued he started to head for home furtively looking in all directions to make sure the coast was clear. He was shaken and yet in a sense he felt a new sense of boldness. He had successfully outrun and outwitted the law.

He got home and went into his room. He pulled the book out from his underwear and laid it on the bed. He changed t-shirts and decided to lay down to recover and think about what had just happened. Somehow in his thought process he decided he needed a gun. A gun would protect him. People were out to get him and all he wanted was to be left alone. He started to consider possible ways of obtaining a gun. He was good at theft now. All he needed was an opportunity. He was confident that such an opportunity would soon present itself. All he had to do was to be ready when opportunity knocked.

A few days later, the opportunity clearly knocked. Cal's anti-social disposition continued become more apparent. He had always been a victim of bullying in school and in the neighborhood. He was a thin, lanky kid and was frequently a subject of physical punches as well as verbal taunts and insults. His confrontation with the law reinforced his disrespect for the law. A gun would protect him. He would get his revenge.

He saw the police car racing down the road in pursuit of a black truck. Suddenly, the police vehicle swerved and hit a light standard. No one else was immediately around. The air bag had deployed. The officer was sitting there unconscious. Cal opened the door and there in front of him was the officer's gun in a holster by the cop's side. Cal had originally wanted to call 911. However, he decided someone else could do that while reaching in to get the gun free. He wiped the door handle with his handkerchief, put the gun down his pants and left the scene. All this happened in only a few seconds, but it seemed like an eternity. People came running up to the car while sirens blared in the distance. No one even noticed the kid on the bike pedaling down the road.

Chapter Ten

Cal sped down the street feeling all-powerful and brave. The gun stuck in the elastic of his Jockey underwear empowered him at long last to feel he could stand up to his enemies. He would no longer

Cower in fear when confronted by the guys in his neighborhood. He could now take care of himself. He was confident that no one saw him. Smiling all the way home, Cal felt bold and smart. These were feelings he was unaccustomed to having.

He got home quickly. His mother was lying passed out on the couch while the TV blared. The telephone lay next to her off the hook and making a buzzing noise. A normal day for Cal. He put the phone back on its receiver. He turned off the TV. Looking at his mom, her mouth open and snoring, Cal felt nothing. He knew she would wake up in an hour or so and stumble to the bathroom oblivious to anything or anyone around her.

Cal shut the door to his room and stared at the gun. He had no experience with weapons. He thought to himself that it couldn't be that hard to shoot because in this area of the city everyone had a gun and knew how to use it. A sudden thought crept into his brain. Bullets. Where could he get the ammo he needed for the gun? He turned and opened the chamber. He saw that there were fifteen bullets. Satisfied that this was a start, he relaxed and smiled. The thought of revenge made his whole-body tingle with excitement. He was confident that getting more ammo wouldn't be a problem.

He was distracted by a loud crash he heard from the next room. He knew it meant that his mother had awoken and on her way to the bathroom had knocked something down. He opened the door and peered out the door. He saw that she had hit a small lamp that stood on the table near the sofa. The lamp was broken. Shards of glass were scattered on the floor. Cal was used to things like this happening. He got out the broom and dustpan and began to clean up the mess. He grumbled to himself that the only cleaning here was what he did. He felt angry that it sometimes seemed as if he were his mother's caregiver.

When she emerged from the bathroom, she merely stared at him with a look of disgust before making her way back to the stained and dirty couch she inhabited. Within minutes she got up and made her way back to the bathroom. Drinking a bottle of Jack Daniels will do that to you.

His thoughts were interrupted by a loud knock at the door. He knew instinctively that it was crazy Eddie from next door. Eddie was one of the ugliest guys one could imagine and had the personality of a rattlesnake. He was also his mom's sometimes lover. Eddie was an ex-con who had shot a store clerk about ten years ago. The clerk survived and Eddie was caught. The clerk recognized Eddie in a police lineup.

Eddie was very often picked up by the police for the lineups. "It must be because I'm so pretty," he laughed. His mood changed when he saw who was looking at the lineup.

Eddie would say that the clerk was extremely stupid. "He should have just given me the money without a fuss," he would say to anyone who would listen. Eddie was aware that the new DA was lenient in judging first time offenders. His confidence was rewarded when he only got a weapons offense and was sentenced to eighteen months in prison plus two years' probation." Prison wasn't too bad", said Eddie. "There are some weird guys there though, so you have to be careful."

Cal suddenly realized that Crazy Eddie was the man to talk to about weapons. He also realized that he had to be careful not to give away the fact that he was in possession of a police gun. He knew Eddie was crazy and would take the gun away from him if he could.

Cal knocked at the bathroom door to announce that Eddie was here. Cal heard a grunting affirmation that she had heard. "Eddie, tell me again about when the police caught you. Boy, I'll bet you were scared when they pointed their guns at you," Cal said.

"Nah, I knew they wouldn't shoot me. Even with those big guns pointed at me, I stood my ground. They only suspected me of shooting the jerk. The guy had such thick glasses that I was sure he couldn't positively identify me."

This was Cal's opportunity to ask about police guns. "What kind of guns did the police have?" Cal asked.

Eddie seemed to light up. He told Cal that the police weapon of choice was Sig Sauer P226. It a long barrel to improve accuracy and was common police side arm. "I wish I could get my hands on one of them. I'd show them," Eddie bellowed. "If you're planning something, be careful. Don't get caught."

Cal's mom came out of the bathroom. Eddie smiled, reached out to her and they went to the couch all the while with Eddie grabbing at her nightgown. It was time for Cal to leave for the rest of the day. He grabbed the gun stuck it into his underwear, pulled down his T-shirt to cover the bulge and headed out the door.

He got on his bike and headed for the woods. He found comfort in hearing the chirping of the birds. He had learned many of the calls and could readily identify the cardinals, blue jays, chickadees and woodpeckers that greeted him. He found great peace in the woods and resented being disturbed by the walkers or birders he encountered. He came to his favorite place in the woods. Short scrub oaks interspersed with saw palmettos and other weedy growth soon surrounded him. This was where the scrub jays lived. They were his jays. He even gave them silly names and was able to identify each individually. Today he saw Big Mo, the family scout, pop out to see who the intruder was entering their territory. That's when he first noticed the intruder. Around the path's curve, stood an older man, maybe fifty years old. Binoculars hung from his neck. His hand was extended. Then he saw one of the jays, Sophie by name, land on the man's head and swoop down to take a peanut. Cal's heart was racing. His face was flushed.

Cal had learned that it was illegal to feed the jays. Feeding them made the birds more vulnerable to predation from hawks. He decided it was his job to protect them. He would do whatever was necessary to keep them safe. As he was watching, other jays from the colony appeared and were eager to get a peanut. Suddenly, Cal saw the hawk swoop down in the scrub to get one of the birds. Fortunately, he missed. His target bird, Brandy by name, had disappeared in the thick underbrush. This had to stop. This was too close for comfort. He ran out and started yelling at the old man. The guy just laughed, turned his back and started to walk away. Cal didn't like being laughed at and this guy was responsible for almost losing one of the Jays.

He wasn't about to allow people like this to harm his birds. He reached into his pants. Carefully, he aimed the gun at the guy who was walking away. Cal pulled the trigger. The old man fell to the ground. Blood was flowing all over the front of his shirt. Cal went over and pulled the body into some thick nearby undergrowth. He reached over and snatched the victim's binoculars. He heard voices coming up the path. He realized he needed to exit the scene immediately. He looked at the body one more time and said to himself, "I could not let you hurt my birds old man."

He thought to himself as he stealthily made his way to his bike that killing a man doing bad things was entirely justifiable. He felt proud of what he had accomplished. The guy deserved it. The birds needed protection. I did what was necessary to keep them safe from idiots who don't obey the law. "I'm sort of a hero," he thought to himself as he pedaled away. I'm a hero just like in those Marvel movies.

Part Three: Detective Nicotra

Chapter Eleven

Eugene Nicotra was ten years old when he decided to become a police officer. He was impressed by the respect and admiration police received. The nuns at his school would praise the police for their bravery. Even the New York Times would run articles noting how the police kept the city safe. Nick, as he was nicknamed, thought being in the police department would be great. Everyone would love and respect him especially the pretty girls. One special girl had caught his eye.

He had first noticed her at a basketball game. His team, the St. Matt's Eagles were playing the St. Pat's Green Dragons. We called them the Greenies. It was the Italians versus the Irish.

Mary Kay was a cheerleader for the Greenies. The dark green skirt and white top she wore made her look like a doll he had once seen in Macy's window. She had reddish blond hair, white porcelain skin, and a broad smile. She was irresistible. At ten years old, Nick could recognize class when he saw it.

Just after graduating high school, Nick asked Mary Kay to be his bride. Mary Kay's family put up some opposition to such a union. The Irish did not marry Italians. "Find yourself a nice Galway lad," her mother pleaded. Nothing could dissuade them and on a beautiful

October day, Nick and Mary Kay were married at St. Pat's. Mary Kay's mom cried through the entire ceremony.

Nick's mom and dad had convinced "Uncle Dom," a distant relative of the family to let the new couple live in an apartment he owned located right in the heart of little Italy. Mary Kay's mother was horrified. She had been hoping the newlyweds would live in the family home with her. The house was very large, having five bedrooms. It was perfect for the new couple. Living in little Italy would be like living in a foreign country. Mary Kay might have to learn to speak Italian! This was an upsetting thought.

Within a couple of months, Mary Kay was pregnant. Nick, meanwhile, had applied to the police academy. His mother and father called on all their connections to make sure he was admitted as soon as possible. Nick was accepted. Nick and Mary Kay were establishing themselves and growing into an irresistible force.

Nick excelled at the Academy. He was one of the top students in his class. After a year's training, Nick was sworn into the department by Mayor Robert Wagner. His family beamed with pride as the twenty-year-old took the oath of office. The new father was now a New York City police officer determined to uphold the law and do honor to his family's name.

His first assignment was as a patrol officer in precinct seven of Brooklyn. This was the area around St. Maria Goretti's parish. It was mostly an Italian area but was changing and becoming more cosmopolitan with black families, Spanish families and other non-identifiable non-Italian residents. Brooklyn was changing. The old clusters of ethnically related people were giving way to new social patterns.

The area was a relatively low crime district. The whole previous year, there were only four murders. They were all domestic incidents. There were some burglaries, a few armed robberies, some shoplifting and of course, plenty of nuisance calls. Nick would have plenty to do in his role of peacekeeper. Nick was loving it!

He loved being a dad too. He would come home each day eager to hear about the day's adventures with little Nick. It wasn't long before Mary Kay was expecting another child.

Nick and his partner, Sgt. Mel Collelli, got along well and were highly respected by the community. They were always ready to lend a helping hand to people in distress. One example was when Nick got out of the patrol car to help an elderly man shovel the snow in front of his brownstone. The old man, about eighty, was breathing hard as he tried to clear his sidewalk. Nick was afraid the gent would have a heart attack, so he stepped in to finish the job.

Marty Mancini had operated his store right across from St. Maria's for almost twenty years. Once in a great while he might catch a shoplifter, but that was about it. Everyone knew Marty and he knew everyone in the neighborhood. On this particular Thursday, he was chatting with Rose Patroni the neighborhood gossip when the young thug came into the shop. He looked around the store seeming to wait for this old dame to leave. She gave him her famous stare and walked out. Marty had a bad feeling about the guy.

Rose saw Nick and Mel cruising down the avenue. She did not hesitate to wave them down. They pulled over and Rose told them this stranger in Mancini's made her uncomfortable. "I didn't like his looks," she said telling them that maybe they should check on Marty.

They got to the store and Mel got out of the car first and walked to the store. Opening the door, he saw the kid holding Marty against a wall pointing his gun at him. The kid told Mel to drop his weapon and to get next to Marty with his hands up. The kid rifled through the cash register filling his pockets with the contents. "You want to live copper then you'll do as I say. Get down on your knees and put your hands behind your back." He hit Mel in the head knocking him out cold. Marty was shaking.

Nick wondered why it was taking Mel so long. He was expecting this to just be Rose's imagination at work. Rose came down the street to speak to Nick. "Everything Okay? She inquired. Nick started to get worried. He told Rose to go home. He got out of the car and began walking slowly to the door. He thought he heard voices from inside. He pulled out his weapon, the first time he ever felt the necessity of pulling out the gun. He stood there momentarily evaluating the situation. Distraction was the trick. If something was going on in there, he would want to confuse the kid and get him to walk to the door to see what was going on. This would give Nick the chance to see what he was up against.

Nick threw a rock through Mancini's store window. The kid ran to peer out the door and Nick pushed the door open and grabbed the kid by the neck forcing him to drop his gun. Marty was shaking and crying at the same time. The backup car arrived. They took the kid away all the while sneering and cursing. Nick rushed to Mel. He had called an ambulance. Mel was starting to come to and was mumbling about something. "You'll be alright," he assured Mel.

Nick was awarded his first medal for bravery. His quick thinking had saved the day and kept everyone safe. There were other awards which followed. Nick advanced in the department to become a detective. Nick and Mary Kay had three other kids in the meantime. His career and family were growing.

He was now head detective for the entire district. His sang-froid in critical, dangerous situations was noticed. The dedication and integrity of his skills made him the best detective in the whole of Brooklyn.

He loved his work. It made him feel like superman. He was keeping the area safe and making sure the bad guys were caught and punished.

The times were changing. Brooklyn was not the same. Crimes were more violent. Murders were way up. Drugs were now common. When he first started his career with the police there were only a few isolated incidents with drug use. Today crime related to drug use or drug sales took up most of his time.

Another change was that the police were no longer regarded as knights in shining armor. Now they were often vilified and criticized. The New York Times seemed to relish publishing articles about police brutality or police corruption. Nick was getting disillusioned. The world of those days early in his career was now often a gritty, dirty place filled with drugs, violence and deprivation.

Paco, as he was called, was a notorious drug lord in most of Brooklyn. He had no morals and no conscience. He and his little group were responsible for a good number of the murders. He had been arrested several times, but with his fancy lawyers was always released. The police it seemed could not get the solid evidence needed to take him off the street and into prison. Nick and Paco were well acquainted with one another. Nick was determined to get him convicted and put away.

Drug dealers don't take kindly to being screwed. Bo Lynn was a young up and coming punk. He'd proved his courage by shooting and killing one of Paco's associates. He also stole the drug stock that Paco had supplied to his boy. A lot of money was involved. More important, however, that this little punk seemed to be challenging Paco's reign over the drug trade in Brooklyn. Paco was going to teach this kid a lesson and end the threat to his turf once and for all.

Bo had managed to attract some joiners. They were all young, mostly teenagers, without morals and mean. They grew up on the streets. They were not afraid of using their weapons to show who was the boss. Nick was aware that there was a new generation of punks in Brooklyn. Punks, with no fear of the police or anyone else. So far, however, the police had, except for several potent skirmishes, avoided a clash that would end with casualties. Nick recognized that he and the other officers were targets and needed to be vigilant.

Officers Barney List and Karen Darrer were on a routine patrol on Bedford Avenue. They knew the area well and were frequent customers at Turkey's Nest Tavern. Barney was quasi-engaged. He had been living with a girl for the last five years. Three years ago, he announced he was engaged. So far, however, everyone, including his girl, was still waiting for the wedding bells to ring. He said he needed time to think.

Officer Darrer became a police officer mainly because her parents were so against it. Her mother secretly was hoping Karen would enter the convent like her sister Pat had done. Her father was planning that she would settle down and find a nice Jewish boy to marry, preferably a doctor. Karen's mom a devout Catholic had fallen in love with Hiram Darrer, the son of a rabbi. Karen was raised in both religious traditions. She joined the force to the chagrin of both parents. At twenty-two, she was a young and inexperienced officer. She was willing to learn how to be a good cop.

Bedford Avenue was the longest street in Brooklyn running all the way to Sheepshead Bay. It was a multiethnic area with many Jewish, some Irish, some black and Hispanic clusters. Brooklyn College was a focal point. College kids were a ready market for the marijuana, Percocet, valium, and harder drugs like heroin that Paco pushed, were popular with many young people. His "salespeople" saturated the campus. The drugs were readily available to an eager consumer base. Paco liked to think of himself as operating the Walmart of drugs. This was a service to his community with "Always low Prices."

Bo wanted a cut from the action and decided after gunning down Paco's boy wonder and obtaining his supplies, that now was the time to make his move and take control of this market. He and six of his followers were heavily armed and ready for action. He convinced himself that Paco's days as drug lord was now history. He was the big man now.

Nick was restless. He needed to take a break deciding to take a long walk down the avenue. It was a beautiful sunny day after a shitty week of rain and cold. He put on his jacket. He needed it to cover his holster. A cop is never far from his gun. Nick was aware of many instances where it was necessary to use it. He also remembered the dire consequences when an officer did not have it with him.

Paco looked out the window and smiled. He lived on the eleventh floor of a nondescript apartment building along the avenue. His neighbors never suspected he was running a full-scale drug operation from it. When Mrs. Rosenbaum questioned him about all the young men who frequented his apartment, he told her that they were all from his church. He replied that he was a deacon there and dedicated himself to counseling these guys. "What a good person you are!" she said smiling.

Paco and three of his troop of "church men" started walking down the avenue towards the college. His "salespeople" were generally hanging around a small shady alcove behind the main building. Paco decided to check on them. He believed that when you get bad vibes you should never ignore them. He just felt like something was up.

Bo with his little band of toughs knew where to look for the "store." Meanwhile, Paco was stopped by Mrs. Rosenbaum who was coming back from the neighborhood bodega. She saw the accompanying group and commented that they were so lucky to have such a mentor. Paco smiled and nodded his head in total agreement. He instructed all, except one of goons to go on ahead. Mrs. Rosenbaum thought how lucky she was to have such a caring person as a neighbor.

Nick was walking briskly. He realized he had gained a lot of weight and was getting a bit flabby in the middle. Sitting all day at a desk or behind the wheel of a car didn't count as exercise. Mary Kay was still as beautiful as the day he married her. He needed to shape up for her sake and for the kids. He didn't want to end up being a fat, old detective who was over the hill. He also harbored an ulterior motive. Reports had reached him that the area around the school was a center of drug activity. He reached the college and immediately noticed these tough looking young guys leaning against a wall. They didn't look like students to him. Two other guys were sitting on a bench with their backpacks open. He saw an occasional exchange of cash between a student and the bench sitters. Nick was hoping to catch Paco in the act of selling drugs. He was thinking about what to do next. He saw Officers List and Darrer approaching the area. Suddenly, the two sellers saw Bo's goons watching them. They picked up their backpacks and decided to leave quickly. It all happened so fast that even Nick was taken aback. Shots were fired. Everyone nearby scattered. Paco's two guys lay on the ground with blood flowing down the path. Officers List and Darrer came running toward the scene. Shots rang out again and Officer List was hit. He was bent over holding his shoulder. Officer Darrer tried to pursue the shooters, but quickly returned to help her fellow officer. Nick pulled out his gun. He had witnessed the whole thing. It was then that he saw Paco.

He was going to get Paco especially after a fellow officer had been shot. Paco boldly stood his ground as Nick approached him. "Something wrong, Detective," he asked. "The streets can be very dangerous these days."

"Put your hands behind your back. You're under arrest" Nick said. Paco had not escaped the shooting. Bo's boys wanted him out of the way. "The streets these days aren't safe for law abiding citizens like me!" More shots rang out coming from down the street as Paco's boys chased the shooters. Soon more officers arrived. Paco was taken into custody.

Nick didn't know how he did it, but he had managed to scare off Paco's entourage. Bo's boys had escaped with the drugs. He and Paco were face to face. Nick ran over to him, took his gun away and waited for more officers and the ambulance to arrive. Officer Darrer seemed to be alright, just a little stunned. Officer List was unconscious but breathing. He seemed to have been hit in the leg. Bo was dead down the street. The smart-ass kid had learned a lesson the hard way. Paco's boys managed to get their revenge.

Nick, fully aware that Paco's sharp lawyers would try to portray him as an innocent bystander who was being intimidated by a corrupt cop. Bo was dead. Paco was feeling more powerful than ever. His shoulder was healing. Mrs. Rosenbaum even sent him a get-well card while he recovered in the hospital. Paco regarded the trial as a nuisance. After planting the story that Nick was a corrupt cop who was not really interested in knocking out these drug sellers. Instead, he wanted a piece of the action. The story appeared in the New York Times.

The Nicotras fought back. It must have been that Sicilian spirit that rose to the occasion. They worked to get the story out about Nick's honesty and valor. He was interviewed on TV and impressed a lot of people. The mayor and police chief stood up for him.

Paco's trial was short and sweet. Nick's testimony was that he witnessed Paco shooting Bo in cold blood. He also testified that he had seen him selling drugs. The verdict came in as guilty on all counts. Paco would never be free again.

Nick woke up in the middle of the night sweating and anxious. He knew he lied. He didn't witness Paco killing Bo and he didn't positively see any drug deal. He calmed down thinking that he still was heroic. It was the only way to get this creep off the street. It was just a fib, but it did a lot of good. Sometimes. He reasoned, lying can be beneficial. Paco's gang was neutralized.

Within a few months, Nick announced his retirement. Mary Kay was tired of the cold and snow and wanted to go to Florida. That sounded good to Nick and before you knew it, they were headed to the sunshine state.

Nick felt he needed a break from the squalor and crime he encountered every day as a detective in Brooklyn. It was time for a change. He would be free of drug dealers, murderers, prostitutes and other lowlifes that filled his day as a detective. He looked forward to sitting by a pool with a Margarita soaking up the Florida sun. He might even take up golf.

They settled into their new home which was situated in a gated senior only community in Central Florida. They decided living on the coast could be a little tricky because of Hurricanes. Before they decided to move there had been a coastal storm that wreaked havoc on homes and businesses there. Besides, if Walt Disney recognized that it was better for his dream park to be built in the center part of the state which was typically protected from hurricanes, then it was better for the Nicotras too.

Moving anywhere is hell. Moving across fifteen hundred miles is even more challenging. They loved their new spacious home and stood in awe at the palm trees that surrounded it. It took awhile involving hard work and a lot of grit, but the move from hell turned into a dream come true. They were home.

Nick golfed a lot. His game improved considerably. Mary Kay joined the Red Hatters, Book Clubs and even a writer's group. After a few months, Nick was getting bored. Their new routine of golf for Nick, club meeting for Mary Kay and lunch at the clubhouse and dinner at someone's home or at a nearby restaurant lacked something. Nick had lived with the danger of being a detective in New York every day for years. He missed the tingle of excitement he got from facing danger and helping people.

He met Sheriff Grady Judd of Polk County. He was impressed. He spoke to the sheriff and discovered that it was possible that a man of his early sixties and in good shape could possibly be considered for the department. Nick's credentials were exemplary. He passed all the physical requirements and became a detective in Polk County. Being a detective here was not the same as being a detective in Brooklyn.

CHAPTER TWELVE

Diane loved living in Florida and was taking full advantage of all the amenities our little paradise provided. In addition to her activities with the Audubon Society, she joined a couple of clubs including a book club. She makes friends easily and while chatting with a woman named Mary Kay. They hit it off immediately. When she found out her name was Mary Kay Nicotra she was stunned. "You're not related to Detective Nicotra? "

I couldn't believe it, never realizing that Detective Nicotra could be one of us living in Paradise Woods. Our development, Paradise Woods, was for retired folks. We had retired early and had been living here for several years. We assumed that everyone else was also retired. I couldn't imagine what it would be like having a tough job like being a detective at that age.

The news of the murder was now old news. After the initial consternation and hysteria, Paradise Woods was back to being a little bit of paradise. The murder in the nature area across from it was forgotten. I still would get a little apprehensive thinking about it. However, it seemed to me that the shooting nearby and the shooting in Osceola County were just random events. They had nothing to do with bird watching and undoubtedly the shooter was long gone from here. The one at the Disney Wilderness Preserve was a wife shooting her husband over an extra marital affair. Bird Watching had nothing to do with it.

A newspaper article tried to link the two shootings, but it was readily recognized that they were totally unconnected. Bird Watchers were probably safe. The shootings represented an aberration that could have occurred anywhere. Crossing a street was probably more dangerous than birding.

Diane was off to one of her club meetings, so I decided it was a good day to get back out in the woods. Nature is always full of unexpected surprises and my year's bird list was especially anemic. The woods across the road was a good place to get some birds. I needed to reach my traditional goal of at least two hundred species a calendar year.

I drove to the area where the shooting had occurred. I admit to feeling a little apprehensive, but it was necessary to put the whole distressing situation behind and get back to birding. The parking area was deserted, so I was able to park under the live oak tree that provided the only shade there. The weather predicted a hot afternoon. I didn't relish the idea of coming back to a steamy car. I needed to overcome my anxiety and get out there to hike and look for birds.

I started down the path and immediately encountered a rafter of turkeys. Seeing me they took off into the underbrush gobbling and complaining about the interruption to their dining on the freshly fallen seed pods. Seeing the comical antics of the birds helped me feel more relaxed about my bird walk.

Walking further down the path, I heard Cardinals, Blue Jays, Chickadees and Titmice. There were woodpeckers, blackbirds and crows. I was in heaven surrounded by the avian friends I loved. This was living at its best. Florida, retirement, a beautiful community and a nearby place to bird made me content and happy to be alive.

Without thinking I was instinctively drawn to the interior area of scrub oak and undergrowth where the Scrub Jays lived. On a low branch in front of me the sentinel bird appeared. He stared at me, probably assessing the situation. Quite possibly, he wondered if I had peanuts with me. I stood still silently watching him.

Curiosity got the best of me. I carefully raised my hand wondering if the bird would come to perch on it even though I didn't have peanuts. The air was filled with a loud bang. I felt the intense pain in my right shoulder and fell to the ground trying to let out a feeble yell for help. That's all I remember. A little voice inside my head kept saying: "I told you so!"

Chapter Thirteen

Robert Hatch grew up in Florida. It is unusual these days to find a real native Floridian. Bob was the real thing. He graduated Haines City high with honors and went on to get a scholarship for UCF. Going to the University of Central Florida meant that he could continue working at Jim Parker's hardware store. Bob loved working there. Jim was a dedicated bird watcher. They would often sit in front of the store waiting for customers. Jim would identify every bird he heard. Bob was a quick learner and soon was able to identify a dozen birds by sound.

Bob saved up enough money to buy an inexpensive starter pair of binoculars. They didn't have the finest optics, but they did open up Bob to a whole new world. Some of the smaller songbirds are difficult to find without binoculars. He was ecstatic the day he first saw a Yellow Throated Warbler. Seeing the vibrant yellow throat contrasted with the black stripe on each side was awe inspiring for him. He was now a dedicated birder.

Graduating with a degree in Elementary Education, he began teaching fourth grade at Emerson Elementary in Auburndale. He met his wife Gladys there. She was the school nurse. Bob developed a pang in his heart upon first seeing her. Because he was lovesick, he would try to visit the nurse's office as often as possible. They were married within the year.

He and Gladys would frequently take long walks in the nearby nature center. She bought some bird guides and binoculars and together they became a dynamic team. Two or three times a week they would bird. They even took long birding vacations. Bird destinations were always included in any vacation plans.

After twenty-eight years of teaching and twenty-nine years of nursing, they both retired. Bob took early retirement. Their son, Bob Jr. and his wife threw a big party to celebrate. Bob and Gladys were now free to bird the world at least as far as their finances allowed.

They loved cruising and were able to combine it with their love of bird watching. A company called Carefree Birding introduced Bob and Gladys to the new bird wonders of the islands. Life for Bob and Gladys couldn't be better. Living in Florida, retirement, and good neighbors and friends made life a dream come true.

Gladys and daughter-in-law, Carmen, were out shopping. Carmen was looking for a party dress. Bob Jr. was to receive an award for the most sales of building supplies from his employer. This was a prestigious achievement for him. The awards dinner was at Flemings Steak House in Orlando. Carmen wanted to look her best and Gladys was anxious to help.

Bob decided it was a good day to go birding. He never missed a chance to head for the nearest birding area. It was a beautiful day. Not too hot with little chance of rain. Perfect! He grabbed his backpack, put in a couple of bottles of water, his binoculars and almost as an after thought, threw in a few peanuts. The weather was perfect. Life was good!

As he approached a curve in the trail, he spied a large kettle of vultures on the ground feeding on the remains of a dead animal. He recognized that it was a mixed group of Black and Turkey Vultures voraciously tearing apart what might have been a possum. Nearby, separate from the feeding frenzy, was a much more interesting bird. A Crested Caracara, with its distinctive colorful face, black crest and black belly, was a great find. He hadn't seen one for a couple years and couldn't wait to tell Gladys.

He soon arrived at his favorite place in the preserve. Sitting on a tree nearby was the sentry. He walked closer and took out his phone to snap a picture. He already possessed dozens of photos of the scrub jays, but this could possibly be the "one." It could turn out to be his premier picture of the jays. He suddenly remembered the peanuts he had thrown in his backpack. "What the hell," he thought to himself, "a few peanuts wouldn't do any harm."

Out of nowhere, a kid appeared, yelling and gesticulating at him. "Stop that," the kid screamed. "Don't you know it's dangerous for the birds. It's stupidity like that which is killing the birds."

Bob didn't respond. He knew it was illegal and potentially harmful to the birds. He smiled at the young man and thought to himself that the kid was correct. He shouldn't be feeding them peanuts. He turned his back to walk away. He took a few steps when he felt it. It was a pain so intense like nothing he had ever felt before. He fell to the ground. Blood was everywhere. He had been on coumadin for years and now was bleeding to death.

The kid ran up to his lifeless body and pulled off his binoculars. Hearing voices coming closer, he dragged the body into the underbrush and ran into the woods. Cal walked off the trail into the woods and underbrush. Hidden from sight he saw the two men. They seemed almost oblivious to the gunshot and were focused on looking at the birds. He headed for the parking area and his bike. It was chained to a small tree. He undid the lock and boarded it. Cautiously, he pedaled away with a smirk on his face.

CHAPTER FOURTEEN

Jake Elder and his younger brother, Dave, were trying to exercise after a challenging week at school. Jake was studying to be a physician's assistant at Gannon University in nearby Reston. Dave was a math major at UCF. They were staying a few days with their Aunt Diane in Paradise Woods. They'd often come to the preserve during their frequent visits there.

They had started down the trail hoping to cover about four miles before the midday heat. It was a gorgeous morning with the temp in the low seventies. A great day for a healthy long walk.

"Did you hear that?" Dave said apprehensively. "It sounded like a gunshot. It was very close." Carefully, they headed ahead from where the sound originated. As they neared a clearing, Jake saw the body on the ground. Standing beside him was a young guy trying to snatch the victim's binoculars. Jake without thinking yelled," Hey, what do you think you're doing?" The skinny guy was holding a pistol. A look of alarm was shown on his face. He ran past Dave and Jake. Pushing Jake to the ground, he dashed into the thick woods and disappeared. Dave was going to give chase, but he felt he needed to help Jake up and see about the guy on the ground.

The guy on the ground was bleeding on left shoulder. Jake began using his training as a P.A. He made a tourniquet out of his T-shirt. He told Dave to run ahead to the parking area and call for an ambulance.

Hopefully, he thought, cell reception would be better there. Jake quickly made a cursory exam of the victim and was confident, now that the bleeding was under control, that the man was going to make it. Jake almost immediately had seen the Medic Alert tag the victim wore around his neck. It was vital to make sure the blood flow was stopped if he was to survive.

It took about fifteen minutes for the ambulance to arrive. The EMT's were followed by several sheriff's deputies. Detectives Nicotra and Smiley arrived on the scene within minutes.

The Sentry Jay sensing danger, ascended from the brush to the top of the tree. His plaintive wheep call warned the other birds of danger in the vicinity. Assessing the situation upon seeing the EMT's wheeling in a stretcher, the sentry flew down to find safety in the thick undergrowth.

Jake and Dave were shaken by the experience. A walk in the woods on a beautiful morning turned into a harrowing event. They watched as the victim was lifted onto the stretcher and taken down the path and disappeared. They soon heard the ambulance siren as it left the parking lot. The two detectives told them to wait. They were anxious to tell the detectives what they saw.

The ambulance sped down Johnson Avenue towards the Poinciana Medical Center where they would stabilize and prepare the patient to be airlifted to a larger hospital. From here a helicopter awaited the ambulance to take the victim to Orlando Hospital in the city. Detective Nicotra had called his wife, Diane, and she was there as well. "He absolutely dreaded the idea of ever flying in a helicopter!" she said to one of the medics.

"It sure seems like the perp is going after bird watchers. The other guy was in the exact area as this. I sure hope this guy makes it," Nick said looking at Smiley. "I just don't understand this at all. I warned Dan that he should be more careful and not be here alone."

CHAPTER FIFTEEN

I hurt all over. The pain in my shoulder was intense like nothing I had ever experienced before. I slowly opened my eyes." Where was I? Why were all these wires sticking in me? What's going on?" I looked around and saw Diane sitting next to the bed.

"Well, it's about time you woke up," she said smiling. "You slept through two whole days!" Now it was coming back. I remembered walking and then everything seemed to go blank. Diane's presence was reassuring and comforting. She stroked my hair and looked angelic. "You're going to be alright. Fortunately, the bullet went into your shoulder and didn't do any significant damage, "she said.

"What bullet? What?' I screamed.

"Don't you remember? You were birding at the preserve, and someone tried to steal your binoculars."

"What! Where are my binoculars?" I was in a panic now. I loved my binoculars. They'd been with me through a lot of birding adventures both here and in many other countries. A person can develop an intense relationship with his glasses. I couldn't bear the thought of losing them. After all, it was through them I saw many of my most desired avians.

The door opened and Detective Nicotra walked in followed by his assistant, Detective Smiley. "Glad to see that you woke up. Didn't I warn you that you should be extremely careful being there. We think the thief is targeting bird watchers and photographers to steal their fancy equipment. We have deputies assigned there to keep an eye out for the perp. Don't worry, will get him very soon now."

A nurse walked in and announced that it was time to clear the room and allow the patient to rest. Nicotra and Smiley looked at each other and turned to leave. Diane gave me a kiss before leaving promising to be back at dinner time. The nurse, Sarah, proceeded to take my vitals before asking if I needed anything. She told me that the doctor would be in later that afternoon.

While laying there, I attempted to recall the events of that morning. I judge my mind was still groggy from the anesthetic that had been used during the surgery. My awareness of time and place had been turned upside down, which made it difficult to remember everything that happened. Losing two days made me confused and dazed. I fell asleep trying to make sense of it all.

Detective Nicotra stopped Diane and told her that their investigation was at a critical point. The two walkers, Jake and Dave, had seen the person trying to steal the binoculars. The detectives were convinced that the murders were about stealing the cameras and optics. There was, however, no attempt to steal my binoculars. They said that the murder in Osceola and the one at the preserve were related. The gun used was the missing police gun stolen from an officer who had been injured in an accident. Unfortunately, there were no witnesses to the gun theft. The officer's body cam had been damaged by the air bag and was useless. Nicotra predicted with an air of confidence that they would find the murderer. He was sure of it.

Jake and Dave were recounting the whole episode to their aunt. She seemed very distressed about the situation. "The world's gone crazy. You can't even go for a peaceful walk in the woods these days," she said as she burst into tears.

Cal was feeling lucky. He didn't get the optics he wanted, but he had succeeded in protecting the Jays from "the idiot people who didn't obey the law about feeding the birds." He was confident that he wasn't recognizable. "The two jerks won't be able to ID me," he thought. He decided to go to the nearest McDonald's and get a giant cheeseburger and lots of fries. Shooting someone made him hungry.

Nicotra had an uneasy feeling. All the evidence pointed towards someone wanting to steal the cameras and such and yet he felt there was more to it. It was said back in New York that he had a sixth sense. As a result, he was able to solve puzzling cases that had unexpected results. Nick's sixth sense had kicked into operation. He would think about it. "Smiley," he yelled, "Let's call it a day and head to O'Brien's for a couple of brews." Grinning broadly, Smiley approved the plan.

Gladys, Bob Jr., Gladys and Bob's only child, and Carmen, Bob Jr's wife, sat in the living room grieving over the tragic death of their husband and father. They were waiting for the arrival of Al O'Connor from the funeral home. Bob's death was completely unexpected. The family was totally unprepared. No one could conceive of a world without the gregarious Bob." What's this world coming to when a birder isn't safe in the woods?" said Gladys. "Bob just loved looking at the birds." Her voice was full of sadness as the tears streamed down her face. Bob Jr. with tears streaming down his face replied that the world had indeed become a dangerous place.

Cal's mother and Eddie were halfway through their second bottle of Crown Royal. Eddie had picked up a pair of bottles from the local bar by giving the bar tender some joint he happened to get out of the pocket of a guy passed out on the street. It was Eddie's lucky day! Being the nice guy that he was, Eddie decided to share it with his woman. He couldn't remember her name, but so what. She supplied what he wanted. What more could a person ask for? Eddie was always a lucky opportunist who took advantage of every opportunity.

Chapter Sixteen

Cal inhaled the cheeseburger and fries. He still felt hungry. He went up to the counter to get another. The girl working behind the counter, Kim, smiled at Cal. It was the kind of smile that invited a response. He had been feeling a little horny lately with all the extra adrenaline flowing through his body. He never had much luck with girls. As a result, he never really tried and managed to take care of himself. Emboldened by his newly found power, he asked the girl if she wanted to get together when her shift ended. "Yea, that be super," she replied.

Kim and Cal ended up behind the trash dumpster at the far end of the back parking lot. It was secluded enough for their rendezvous with lust. They parted and Cal promised to be back soon. Cal was in love or was it something else? He got on his bike and sped off. He felt different. He had proven his manhood today. He felt invincible.

Cal raced home. Traffic was heavy, but he managed to fly around the slow-moving vehicles to get home. He chained the bike up next to the streetlight that had not illuminated anything for years. The poor end of town seldom got any attention from the city manager.

He headed up to his mother's sixth floor apartment. Royal Oaks was anything but royal. Even the live oaks around the building looked beat up without the stature of those in the city parks. Everything about Royal Oaks was disgusting. The outside concrete needed a paint job. It had never been repainted in the nearly twenty years that the building had stood at the corner of Fourteenth and Reed Streets. This was the part of town anyone with good sense would avoid. Drugs, prostitution and crime were the area's exports.

The elevator was working again after being inoperable for almost a month. Cal still felt wary whenever he used it. It made a strange grunting sound when moving and it seemed to growl when it was to stop. Cal made it safely to apartment 601.

As he turned the key, he heard voices from inside. They were loud and angry. He opened the door. There stood Crazy Eddie in his tattered and dirty Jockey briefs. He was holding a bottle of whiskey and yelling at Cal's mother. She lay on the sofa wearing her bra and panties. She looked angry.

"Give me the bottle," she pleaded. "You promised to share."

Crazy Eddie laughed. He turned to see Cal standing there. "What the hell do you want boy! Go away, we're busy," he sneered. His toothless smile made him look somewhat intimidating. Cal thought he looked like those pirates he saw in that movie a couple of years ago.

"What's that bulge in your pocket, boy," he snorted. Laughing to himself he said, "I know what it ain't. You ain't man enough to get one that big!"

Cal tried to ignore Eddie's insult. Whenever he felt angry, he would think about the birds he loved. He pictured a Painted Bunting pecking the ground for seeds. He headed to his room with that thought in mind when suddenly Crazy Eddie grabbed him from behind. His hand reached into Cal's underwear and pulled out the gun. He tried to stop him. Eddie punched him hard in the mouth. Cal lay on the ground.

Eddie was admiring the gun when Cal suddenly re-invigorated, jumped up and tried to swipe the gun away. They wrestled on the floor with Cal trying to grab hold of the gun. Eddie, who was bigger and stronger, had the upper hand. Cal was determined and unrelenting in his effort to regain control of the gun.

Then it happened. A shot exploded in the air. Cal's mother let out a loud wail. Eddie stood up. He was holding the gun. Cal lay on the ground with blood flowing on the floor. Eddie opened the door and ran. He flew down the emergency steps. Down six floors and flew out the back door. He threw the gun into the trash bin. He was experienced enough to wipe the weapon clean of his prints.

Old Man Charlie, who lived in apartment 602 was scared. He heard the gunshot. It was not that unusual to hear shots, but this one sounded too close. He dialed 911 to report a shooting.

The sheriff arrived within ten minutes of Charlie's call. It was an area that law enforcement was very familiar with. The ambulance followed right behind. The EMT's dashed up and attended to Cal. He was still breathing but unconscious. They lifted him on the stretcher and rapidly took him down the elevator and into the ambulance. Sirens blared as it sped away toward the hospital.

Detectives Nicotra and Smiley arrived on the scene. Forensics was already there and gathering evidence. Cal's mother was hysterically screaming "Eddie did it. He killed my son."

Nick told her that Cal was not deceased and was being taken to a hospital. "Who is this, Eddie? What's his full name?"

Cal's mother had no idea and could not provide much more information. Smiley, Nick's partner was interviewing neighbors. He found out that there was an Eddie who lived in apartment 604. No one knew much about him except that everyone called him Crazy Eddie.

"He was really a creepy guy," Old Charlie said. "He reminded me of a snake. Poisonous and dangerous."

Nicotra and Smiley had their hands full with another serious case.

CHAPTER SEVENTEEN

The detectives arrived at headquarters and began the process of gathering all the information on the case. The murder investigation took priority, but the shooting at Royal Oaks was also on their minds. Forensics had reportedly found a gun in the trash bin behind the apartment building. They did not find any prints on it, but had discovered something important enough for Lynn O'Malley, the head of the Forensics Department, to come to see Nicotra in person.

"The gun we found was used in the shooting and was the same one stolen from Officer Oakley who was in that car accident a few weeks ago. The chief was very concerned that it would end up in the wrong hands and it appears that it had." O'Malley handed Nick the complete report of all the information gathered from the apartment. There were partial prints on it that were impossible to use for identification. We have reports that the woman's kid lived with her. Eddie, who lived in an apartment nearby, was frequently a visitor. We found his prints in the apartment. He has a police record and spent a year in prison for beating up his uncle over drugs. We also ascertained that this was the gun used in the murder of Robert Hatch, the murder in Osceola County and the most recent wounding of the guy in the preserve." Lynn smiled. She was confident this evidence would help solve the case.

"Thanks," Nick was pleased. "Let's get the son of a bitch!" The entire department was alerted to find Crazy Eddie. "Let's go," he said to Smiley. "I have an idea."

"We will be releasing you this afternoon," Dr. Watkins said smiling. "You were very lucky and the bullet missed an artery. Because you are taking a blood thinner, the wound would have probably been fatal if it was a fraction of an inch closer to the artery. Be sure to buy a lottery ticket. I think you're sure to win with your luck."

Diane was relieved and had a broad smile on her face. "You are absolutely going to take it easy for the next few days!" she ordered.

Both Corgis were exuberant over my return home. It was a wonderful feeling to be alive and home with my beautiful Diane and my two canine buddies. Life is good!

Jerry called later. He jokingly asked if I wanted to go bird watching with him. "Not today," I responded, "but soon."

We hadn't heard any news on the investigation. We were confident that Detective Nicotra would find out who was shooting the bird watchers.

Cal lay in his bed still unconscious. He was still listed as being in critical condition though he was beginning to show some significant improvement. He had no visitors. A nurse was on constant duty monitoring Cal's vitals. She thought that the young man laying there was very lucky to be alive. "It's sad that he's all alone," she whispered to herself.

Eddie was three blocks away in an alley looking for Blaze, a drug dealer whose territory this was. Blaze was a tough looking redhead. She was one of an elite, rare group of female drug lords. If you were wise, you would not mess with Blaze. She ruled her kingdom with an iron hand. Her lackeys took care to make sure the Queen was always respected.

Blaze liked Crazy Eddie. He'd done business with her many times and ingratiated himself by being an informer. Eddie, as crazy as he was, became invisible to most people. He heard conversations, saw comings and goings, and as a result could be a font of information. Information was vital in Blaze's domain.

She soon returned to her "store" location surrounded by her crew of ugly looking behemoths. She was always pleased to see Eddie.

He was feeling extremely anxious as he told Blaze what had just happened. Blaze, he thought, would know what to do. She was smart and tough. Blaze would take care of him.

"Get him some new clothes. Drive him to Parker's old house. He can stay in their garage for a few days till we can arrange transportation out of the state."

She looked at Eddie with a scowl on her face, "You really know how to screw up, don't you? I don't want you to come around here again. We don't need those asshole detectives coming around here. We'll get you out of here, but then you're on your own."

"Thanks," said Eddie as he followed her lackey down the street.

Eddie was dropped off at the garage. They gave him a pillow and a blanket with instructions to stay hidden until further notice. Eddie was not pleased with the accommodations. The place stunk and had bugs. At least in his old place, he didn't have roaches.

He fell asleep thinking about what he needed to do. When he woke up, he decided that he couldn't wait anymore and needed to get away from here as quickly as possible.

CHAPTER EIGHTEEN

The Jays were feasting on a fresh crop of acorns. One of the birds had managed to snag a very large lizard. The sentry, always on duty, heard footsteps coming toward them. He warned the others who instantly took cover while the sentry flew to the top of a nearby oak to view the situation.

Edna Byrd loved birds. She was in Florida shopping for a new home in a place that wouldn't be covered by snow in the winter. Paradise Woods looked very welcoming to Edith. She was a retired spinster schoolteacher from Kansas. She had never lived anyplace else, but her parent's home in Lindsborg Kansas," the friendliest small town in the country" or so the town portrayed itself. In fact, until this trip she had never left Kansas. There weren't any birds left in Kansas she hadn't seen. She decided it was time for her to figuratively spread her wings and move.

She had read about Scrub Jays and desperately wanted to add the species to her life list. Scanning the scrub, she spotted it. The sentry bird looked down from its perch, seemed to appraise the situation as safe and called out"ra/eck, ra/eck" to assure the others that it was safe.

Edna was excited. This was her fourth life bird of the day. She knew she would love living in Florida! As she stood there jotting down her notes on the bird, two men seemed to appear from out of nowhere. Dressed in jeans and polo shirts, Detectives Nicotra and Smiley appeared to be regular birders enjoying nature. Nick's idea was that Crazy Eddie might head back to hide out in the preserve. Nick didn't want to alarm the lady but wanted to gently remind her to be careful walking in the woods by herself. Edna didn't appear ruffled by the suggestion. She felt quite capable of taking care of herself. After all, she had handled two-hundred-pound football players in her high school English class. If circumstances required these big guys would cower when she stood by them.

Smiley suggested to Nick that it was time to move on from the preserve. "I don't think Eddie would be crazy enough to come back here."

Trying to decide what to do next, Nick was unsure of his next move. His phone rang, breaking the silence of the woods. There had been a report that an officer on duty as a school crossing guard had seen someone who looked like Eddie getting in a blue Toyota on Eighteenth Street. The officer was astute enough to take down the license as TPX-653.

"Find out who the car is registered to and let me know quick," screamed Nicotra.

A few minutes later Nick found out that the car had been reported stolen a couple of days ago. Harvey Zinn, a pharmacist at a Walgreen's on fourteenth Street was the owner. He was at work last Thursday and when his shift was over, he discovered the car was gone.

"I want everyone looking for that car." Nick's adrenaline was at max. He was convinced Eddie was going to be in custody before the day was done.

It had been years since Eddie had driven a car. He never possessed a driver's license, nor did he ever take driving lessons. The car was just sitting in the empty lot. He was desperate to get as far away from here as was humanly possible. "I can drive this," he told himself. It was relatively easy to steal it. He drove out of the lot as quickly as possible. Not quite comfortable behind the wheel, he slammed on the brakes lurching him forward. "I've got to use my seatbelt. Don't want any cop after me," he figured. He saw the cop with the stop sign directing kids across the street. Again, he slammed on the brakes so hard everyone around him noticed. He opened the door and got out of the vehicle to make sure he didn't damage the tires. The cop kept staring at this weird driver.

Eddie got back in the car and when it was clear of kids continued down the street. Shaking, he didn't have a destination in mind. Eighteenth street was a major artery and he felt it would lead to an interstate. Oblivious to speed limits he focused on getting away.

Officers Tate and Fields were on routine patrol when they saw the blue Toyota zoom past. They called in their sighting and were instructed to follow the car. Soon other units also responded. Nick and Smiley went to the front of the pack behind Eddie.

"Let's get him," Nick told the patrols. He put on his light and closed in on the car. Eddie finally noticed all the police vehicles behind and in front of him. One of the cops pulled his car across the road blocking access. Eddie jammed on the brakes, opened the door and ran. He ran and ran. Nick and Smiley were in hot pursuit.

Smiley got to Eddie first and pulled him down. Nick, out of breath, grabbed Eddie's hands and put the cuffs on. Eddie was crying.

CHAPTER NINETEEN

The two birds were busy gathering twigs and building a nest under the leafy vine covering the scrub oak. They were constantly flying back and forth adding to the nest structure. One of the birds focused on forming the twigs into a circle in the middle of the nest. The other bird would frequently return and feed this bird an acorn or an insect unlucky enough to be nearby. All the other birds would occasionally come close as if supervising the new avian structure.

Cal who had recently been released from the hospital was watching. He was pleased that in his absence all the birds were safe. Cal felt miserable. His body was still sore and weak. The short bike ride from his home was a challenge. He was aware that in the short time he was recovering, traffic on the road had increased tremendously. Many of the old orange groves were gone almost overnight. In their place were new developments with homes crammed together. The old country road was now becoming a major thoroughfare.

Cal and his mother were to be witnesses in Eddie's upcoming trial. Cal was naturally extremely apprehensive about having to testify about Eddie possessing a gun. Cal's mother, who frequently was foggy about remembering her name, was to be an important witness. The local prosecutor had taken their depositions and was preparing them as witnesses. Nick was trying to convince himself that Eddie was responsible for both murders and the wounding of Dan. All the evidence seemed to point to Eddie.

One detail troubled Nick. He seemed uncomfortable with the presumed motive. Eddie didn't seem smart enough. Nick had a sixth sense that told him something was wrong.

The trial began a few weeks later. The prosecutor had made sure Cal's mother was sober and cleaned up. The county had even paid for a new dress and haircut for her. Cal had never seen his mother look so good.

As expected, the trial was short and sweet. Eddie was found guilty of murder in the second degree. He escaped capital murder charges only because he appeared intellectually impaired. He was sentenced to life imprison.

Nick and Smiley were relieved and in a celebratory mood. The successful conclusion of a case and the subsequent guilty verdict required a trip to their favorite bar.

The prosecutor was also pleased. The case proceeded flawlessly to the desired guilty verdict. "I'm really good" he thought. "The county is safer because of me!"

The funeral for Robert Hatch was held a few weeks before the trial began. Father Ortega had spoken of Bob's generosity and kindness. He was respected and well liked by his former students, many of them attended the service. It was a beautiful service that ended with Bob's favorite hymn, How Great Thou Art!

Bob's widow was still in mourning. It would take a very long time before she could smile again.

Diane and I left the courthouse relieved that the nightmare was over at last. Eddie was not going to shoot at birdwatchers ever again. They could go back into isolated wooded preserves in relative safety. We would always be a little more cautious and wary as a result of this experience.

Why waste a beautiful afternoon? We decided to take a walk through the preserve knowing full well. that the birds are least active at midday. However, you never know. There can always be surprises when birding. Today seemed like our lucky day!

We always kept our binoculars in the car ready to use if an interesting bird should appear. Last week, for instance, in the mall parking lot appeared a flock of Cedar Waxwings chattering loudly in one of the nearby Live Oaks. When we arrived, we saw that the parking lot was almost full. The shady spots were all taken, forcing us to park in a very sunny area. The car would be hot when we returned. That was a small cost for enjoying a beautiful Florida afternoon.

Despite the afternoon heat, we did manage to have a decent bird watching experience. The Blue Jays, Cardinals, Titmice and Catbirds all cooperated to make our fears of being at the preserve melt away. Eddie would never bother nature lovers again!

CHAPTER TWENTY

s a person ages, time seems to speed up so that a year seems like a few weeks. It had been a year since the whole mess began at the preserve. Time also has a way of easing the memories of all that happened. I regained my complete mobility and use of my arm. I also regained my confidence and was more relaxed when by myself walking the trails.

Detective Nicotra was kept busy with an array of crimes, but none as serious as last year's murders. Detective Smiley was awarded a commendation for his bravery in apprehending a wanted felon. Nick, however, occasionally would have a feeling that something was wrong about that murder case. Eddie, the convicted murderer just did not seem to be smart enough or mobile enough to have committed those crimes. Something was not right, he thought. Smiley would always reassure him. "Eddie did it," he would say, "there's no doubt about it."

Gladys Hatch was still not fully recovered from the murder of her beloved husband. The tears were not visible but were internalized. Each evening before retiring she would stop and look at the picture of Bob that stood on the dresser. Each day the mourning continued but became invisible to others.

Cal was completely enthralled by the birds. Even though his reading ability was limited, he would page through his bird guides and try to decipher the commentary associated with the bird photo. He found out that there was a bird club that held a monthly meeting at the library. He decided to join.

The club was led by Sandy Barr and had twelve other members. They would get together every third Monday to share recent observations and discuss environmental issues. Most of the members were retired senior citizens. Two of the group were younger women who lived in a nearby sub-division. Cal stood out. His disheveled appearance and his basic lack of social skills were readily apparent. Birders though, are accepting and welcoming to all. They were eager to welcome Cal to their group.

Cal's mother was back to normal. Jack Daniel's was her best friend. The new dress she had been given for the trial now had stains and was filthy. She spent most of the day sitting on the couch with the TV blaring. She missed Eddie and was sorry she had to testify against him.

Almost every day, Cal would go looking for birds. He especially liked his Scrub Jays. He would spend hours in the area of the preserve where they lived. He could identify each member individually by their newly acquired bands. He gave each bird a name. They were his only real friends.

He was upset when he discovered one day a pile of Jay feathers on the ground near where he always stood watching the birds. His bird, Tommy, was gone. Tommy was a young bird that Cal was especially fond of because he was bold and easily observed. Whenever Cal arrived there, Tommy was always popping out from the underbrush and would fly very near to where he was standing. Suddenly it dawned on him. Tommy's boldness was a result of being fed by someone. That person was responsible for killing Tommy. "I'll make sure that doesn't happen again, Tommy. I'll protect the rest of your family," Cal vowed with tears in his eyes and a quivering voice.

At the next club meeting, Cal shared his grief over the loss of the Jay. "We've got to do something to protect them," he pleaded. Everyone in the club agreed and it was decided that the group would pay to erect signs that read "No feeding the Scrub Jays."

Cal and a couple of the club members spent one Saturday morning putting up the signs. He was proud of himself for being a concerned and active protector of the birds. He was a good citizen!

CHAPTER TWENTY-ONE

Tommy Nolan always wanted to be a fireman. He quit college in his sophomore year after he was accepted for the Polk County Fire Rescue Department. Tommy thought this was a lot better than becoming an accountant. He was a lifeguard, trained in martial arts, and had basic medical training. He started in junior high and had distinguished himself with several awards in martial arts and as a lifeguard. With his martial arts training, he wanted a career that was active and exciting. Accountants spent their time in dull offices. He felt that the fire rescue department was where he belonged. He was assigned to a small station adjacent to the Paradise Woods senior community.

He loved it there. These were the typical calls expected in a senior community. Falls, heart attacks, kidney stones were usual ailments for the medics. Tommy, trained in medical procedures, was the driver of the fire engine that would accompany each medical call. This was standard procedure for the county. There were very few fires. Once in awhile there was a grass fire or a fire in some of the forested areas nearby. House fires were extremely rare. Lightning strikes were often the cause of these fires and Florida was the lightning capital of the world. He knew there would always be a need for his skills.

Tommy was also an avid naturalist. He loved hiking in the woods and would frequently hike with his fiancé, Jenny, somewhere in the woods. He knew the birds, the animals, even the dragon flies he encountered. Curious about everything, he was truly fascinated by all the natural wonders he experienced. He was constantly studying some book about nature. His buddies in the department would tease him that he was a walking encyclopedia of natural history. They nicknamed him Mr. Bird!

Every Wednesday, his day off, Mr. Bird would head for the woods. Most of the time his sweetheart and future wife would accompany him on these outings. Jenny was Activities Director at Paradise Woods. This week, however, she had to work so he was on his own. Tommy decided to go to the nearby preserve to hike and enjoy the warm weather. He packed his backpack with a couple bottles of water, a couple of protein bars and through in a handful of peanuts. Today was going to be a very special day. After being engaged for over eight months, he and Jenny were going to meet at dinner and set the date for their wedding. He would get a few miles in, get showered, put on his best clothes and meet her at Arabellas, a restaurant they both loved.

He arrived at the preserve to find it empty. There was a bicycle chained to a small tree but other than that no one was there. Tommy expected it to be totally peaceful and serene.

Reaching the scrubby area where the Jays lived, he decided to eat one of the protein bars and have a bottle of water. The curious and opportunistic Jays exposed themselves and Tommy laughed at their antics. He remembered the peanuts in his backpack and despite the signs that said NO FEEDING THE BIRDS, Tommy couldn't resist and held out his hand full of peanuts.

Cal who was hidden in a thicket of dense vegetation was furious. As he stood his rage grew and grew. He no longer possessed a gun, but he was not going to allow this jerk to feed his birds. He wouldn't allow them to be endangered as a result of the stupidity of people who disregarded the nearby sign. Cal picked up a large rock that he found on the ground and sprung from his hiding place with his hand raised ready to smash Tommy's head to pieces.

Tommy turned around, saw Cal coming toward him and instinctively put his martial arts skills right to work. Cal did manage to hit Tommy in the back, but Tommy's skills saved him. Cal lay on the ground unconscious. Tommy managed to press the emergency button on his phone. He hoped that the call went through. His neck and back ached. He tried to walk back to the parking area. The pain was intense as he stumbled and lay on the ground.

The ambulance got there first, even beating the sheriff's vehicle. Nicotra and Smiley arrived shortly after they heard the call of an incident at the preserve.

Tommy was placed on a stretcher and his buddies from the station were taking especially good care of Mr. Bird.

The deputies had cuffed Cal. Tommy had managed to tell them what had happened. Cal was enraged.

"That asshole was going to kill my birds. I protect my birds and won't let stupid people hurt them. I did it before and I'll do it again!" Nick and Smiley looked at each other and both knew what Cal had just confessed to committing the other shootings.

At the station, Cal bragged about what he had done to protect his birds. He was sure this made it alright.

Cal's trial was held later that year. He was found guilty and sentenced to life imprisonment.

Eddie was released from prison and received one hundred and fifty thousand dollars in compensation for being in prison. He ended up going back to the Royal Arms and resuming his affair with Cal's mother. A hundred and fifty thousand would pay for a lot of Jack Daniels.

Nick's doubts about the first trial were justified. He felt that Cal's motivation explained everything. In Nick's mind this was truly the conclusion of what they called the Scrub Jay Murders.

Tommy was released from the hospital the next day. Jenny and he set the date. There was a lot to look forward to in the next few weeks preparing for their big day.

Paradise Woods was having an oldies concert with the remaining members of the Beach Boys. Diane and Dan, Jerry, and Nick and his wife were looking forward to a great Saturday night.

The newly hatched babies caused the Jay clan to share in the feeding and protection of the young. Out of the six eggs, four had hatched. Four babies were a feeding challenge and all the birds in the clan were up to the task.

It was another day in paradise.